Y0-BBE-828

GREAT DISCOVERIES IN SCIENCE
Antibiotics

Jonathan S. Adams

Cavendish Square
New York

Published in 2018 by Cavendish Square Publishing, LLC
243 5th Avenue, Suite 136, New York, NY 10016

Copyright © 2018 by Cavendish Square Publishing, LLC

First Edition

No part of this publication may be reproduced, stored in a retrieval system, or transmitted in any form or by any means—electronic, mechanical, photocopying, recording, or otherwise—without the prior permission of the copyright owner. Request for permission should be addressed to Permissions, Cavendish Square Publishing, 243 5th Avenue, Suite 136, New York, NY 10016.
Tel (877) 980-4450; fax (877) 980-4454.

Website: cavendishsq.com

This publication represents the opinions and views of the author based on his or her personal experience, knowledge, and research. The information in this book serves as a general guide only. The author and publisher have used their best efforts in preparing this book and disclaim liability rising directly or indirectly from the use and application of this book.

CPSIA Compliance Information: Batch #CS17CSQ

All websites were available and accurate when this book was sent to press.

Library of Congress Cataloging-in-Publication Data

Names: Adams, Jonathan S., 1961-
Title: Antibiotics / Jonathan S. Adams.
Description: New York : Cavendish Square Publishing, [2018] | Series: Great discoveries in science | Includes bibliographical references and index.
Identifiers: LCCN 2016055340 (print) | LCCN 2016058116 (ebook) | ISBN 9781502628732 (library bound) | ISBN 9781502628749 (E-book)
Subjects: LCSH: Antibiotics. | Communicable diseases--Treatment. | Penicillin.
Classification: LCC RM265 .A33 2018 (print) | LCC RM265 (ebook) | DDC 615.7/922--dc23
LC record available at https://lccn.loc.gov/2016055340

Editorial Director: David McNamara
Editor: Caitlyn Miller
Copy Editor: Michele Suchomel-Casey
Associate Art Director: Amy Greenan
Designer: Lindsey Auten
Production Coordinator: Karol Szymczuk
Photo Research: J8 Media

The photographs in this book are used by permission and through the courtesy of: Cover Science Photo/Shutterstock.com; p. 3 Mediscan/Alamy Stock Photo; p. 5 Fusebulb/Shutterstock.com; pp. 8, 13 DEA Picture Library/De Agostini Picture Library/Getty Images; p. 10 ©Museums Sheffield/Bridgeman Images; p. 11 Academie Nationale de Medecine, Paris, France/Archives Charmet/Bridgeman Images; p. 12 Bloomberg/Getty Images; p. 15 Phil Degginger/The Image Bank/Getty Images; p. 17 John Tyndall's commissioned drawer (anon)/Wikimedia Commons/File:TyndallsSetupForBrothsInOpticallyPureAir(Dated1876).jpg/CCO; p. 20 Hulton Deutsch/Corbis Historical/Getty Images; pp. 21, 25, 35, 49 Bettmann/Getty Images; p. 22 Photo 22/Universal Images Group/Getty Images; p. 26 Baron/Hulton Archive/Getty Images; p. 29 Universal Images Group/Getty Images; p. 31 Print Collector/Hulton Archive/Getty Images; p. 32 Mary Evans Picture Library/Alamy Stock Photo; p. 34 St. Marys Hospital Medical School/Science Photo Library/Getty Images; p.38 Fernando Real/Wikimedia Commons/File:Sir William Dunn School of Pathology, Oxford, 1994.jpg/CC BY-SA 4.0; p. 39 Carroll Siskind/Science Source/Getty Images; p. 42 Daily Herald Archive/SSPL/Getty Images; p. 43 Maximilian Stock Ltd./The Image Bank/Getty Images; p. 45 Yannick Tylle/Corbis Documentary/Getty Images; p. 46 AP Images; p. 48 Xurxo Lobato/Cover/Getty Images; p. 51 Pasieka/Science Photo Library/Getty Images; p. 52 Science Photo Library/Getty Images; pp. 53, 54 BSIP/Universal Images Group/Getty Images.

Printed in the United States of America

Contents

Introduction: Medical Miracles	5
Chapter 1: The Problem of Infectious Disease	9
Chapter 2: "Life Hinders Life"	29
Chapter 3: Major Players in the Discovery of Antibiotics	49
Chapter 4: The Discovery of Penicillin	67
Chapter 5: A Post-Antibiotic Era?	89
Chronology	112
Glossary	116
Further Information	119
Bibliography	121
Index	124
About the Author	128

Before antibiotics, hospital wards like this one in 1890 sought to relieve suffering but offered few cures for common diseases.

Introduction: Medical Miracles

The discovery of **antibiotics**, perhaps the most momentous discovery in the history of medicine, did not come about because of something dramatic that a brilliant scientist did. The discovery of an effective way to fight the deadly infections that plague humankind came about largely because of something that scientist did not do.

In 1928, Alexander Fleming went on vacation. That was not surprising; he earned a good living treating patients in addition to his laboratory research at Saint Mary's Hospital in London, and he loved to putter around the garden of his country house. But the world would have been a far different and far more dangerous place had he decided instead to remain in his cluttered laboratory and keep on working.

What Alexander Fleming found when he returned to London changed the world more dramatically than any other medical discovery. But it did not come out of nowhere, and it did not happen in a brilliant flash of insight that revealed a previously unknown reality. In fact, it was a discovery that was decades, even centuries, in the making, and it would take more than a decade of painstaking, incremental problem solving to move what Fleming saw that autumn day from the laboratory bench to the hospital ward.

It is not unreasonable to divide all of human history in two, before the discovery of antibiotics and after. The world before antibiotics is so foreign to us now that it is almost impossible to imagine. Then, the simplest, most insignificant event could prove deadly: the prick of a pin or the scratch of a thorn. Wars killed millions, not because of the wounds suffered in battle, but because of the infections that followed. Hospitals, far from being places where people went to recover from their illness with the help of the most sophisticated medical science, were places that people went to die.

Antibiotics changed all that. They were the true miracle drugs, the magic bullets. Their discovery, however, came about almost entirely by accident, a series of fortunate events that saved countless lives but could just as easily have led down another of the many dead ends scientists pursued during the long search for a weapon to fight the microbes that cause disease.

The story does not begin or end with Alexander Fleming. In fact, Fleming himself plays a crucial but relatively small role. The story actually begins in ancient societies like Jordan and China, when people realized that eating a particular plant could treat illness or that rubbing a particular type of soil on your skin could treat an infection.

The story continues in Holland in 1675. A tradesman and scientist named Antonie van Leeuwenhoek wanted a better look at the tiny threads he used in his draper's shop, so he cobbled together a homemade instrument with a metal tube and a powerful glass lens he made himself. Pleased with the result, he began looking at other things, such as his own tears. He saw, to his horror and amazement, that he shared his body with millions of tiny creatures that no one had ever seen before. He called them *animalcules*, Latin for "tiny animals." We know them today as **bacteria**.

More than a century later, in England, milkmaids on occasion developed pustules on their hands after touching the udders of cows infected with a mild illness called cowpox. Far more important, milkmaids who had come down with cowpox were immune to a related disease, smallpox, which was the leading killer of the day. Edward Jenner, a physician, postulated that if he took the pus from a cowpox lesion and injected it into a healthy person, that person would get slightly ill but would thereafter be immune to smallpox. He was right, and **vaccines** were born.

Jenner invented a vaccine but he did not know why it worked. That discovery would take nearly another century, when Louis Pasteur realized that if he weakened but did not kill bacteria he could protect against later infection. That advance, together with another just a few years later proving that bacteria and **viruses** were the cause of disease, was the final building block for modern medical science. The stage was set for antibiotics to make their accidental appearance in Alexander Fleming's laboratory.

Fleming's genius was to understand he had found something remarkable, and he refused to give up. But he was unable to take the next step and transform his discovery into lifesaving medicine. That would come more than ten years later through the diligence and insight of three mismatched scientists: Howard Florey, Ernst Chain, and Norman Heatley.

The story of the discovery of antibiotics is as dramatic and important as any in the history of science.

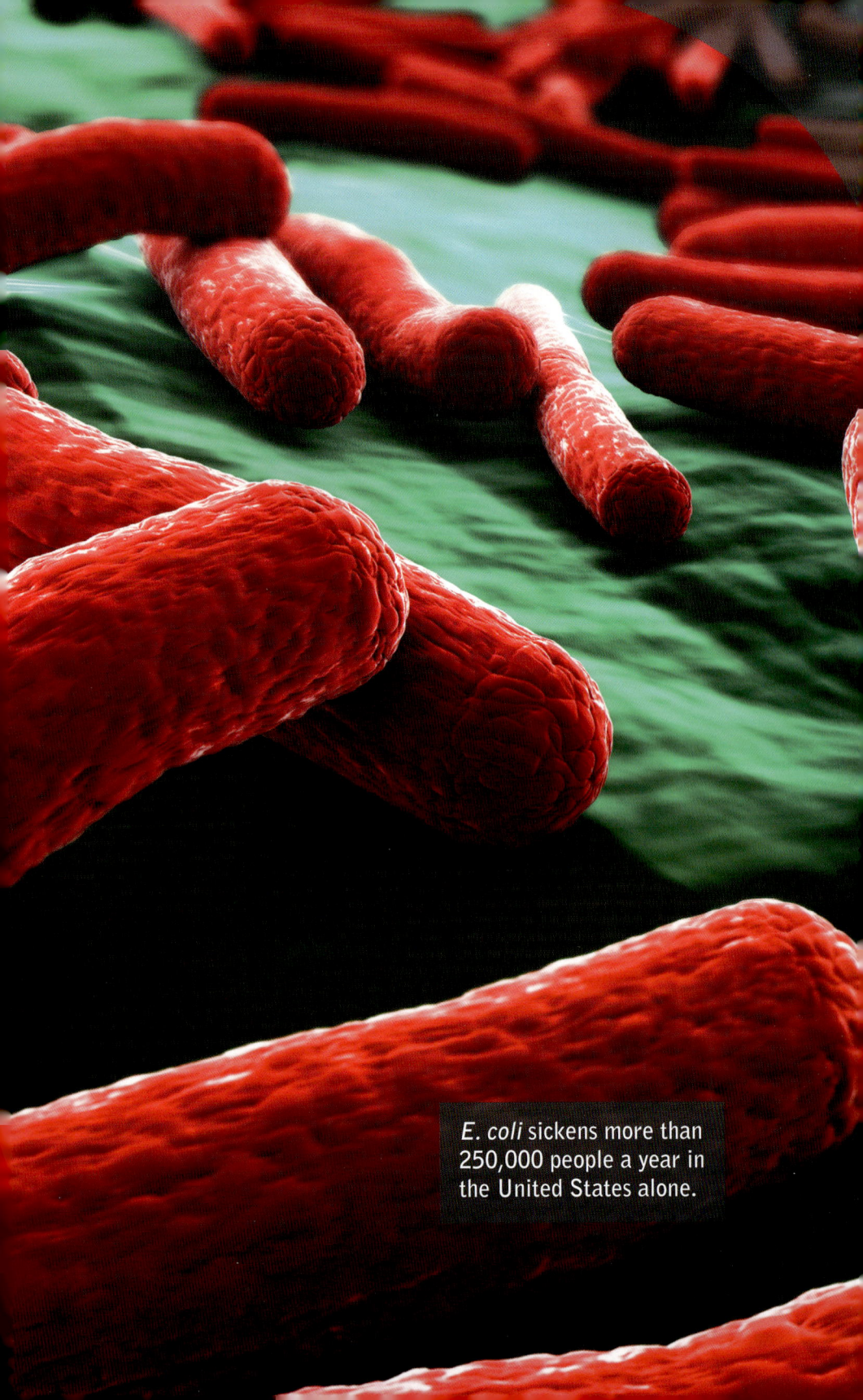

E. coli sickens more than 250,000 people a year in the United States alone.

CHAPTER 1

The Problem of Infectious Disease

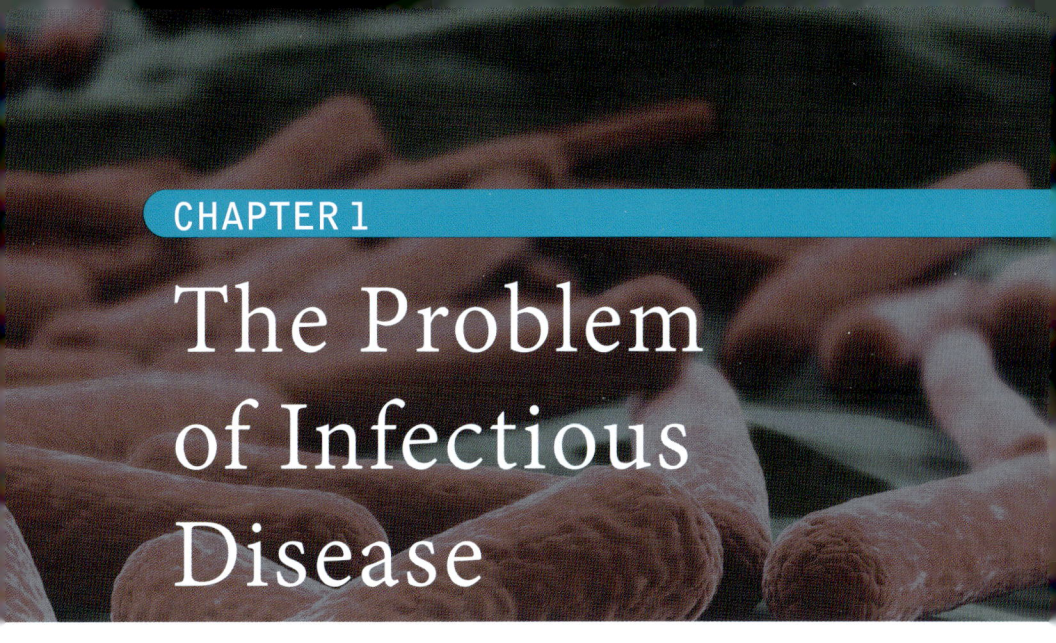

Imagine a world where the slightest accident or the mildest illness could quickly turn into a life-threatening or even fatal crisis: the nick of a blade, a skinned knee, a scratchy throat. Mothers regularly died from infection following childbirth. Epidemics could empty entire landscapes of people. Now, imagine that doctors are almost completely powerless to do anything once an infection establishes itself.

It is nearly impossible to cast ourselves back to the time before antibiotics, an era that lasted from the dawn of human history to less than a century ago. That is how completely, it seems, modern science has conquered the problem of infectious diseases. Actually, there are two important things wrong with the perception that infections were only recently conquered and are now solved by antibiotics. First of all, people learned techniques to prevent fatal infections long before modern science explained the causes of such infections and how the human body responds to them. Second, the battle is in no way at an end. Infections continue to trouble us and likely will do so as long as we share this planet with the seemingly infinite variety of life.

EARLY UNDERSTANDINGS (AND MISUNDERSTANDINGS)

The vast majority of organisms that make up that variety of life remained invisible to humans for the bulk of our existence. The source of illness was mysterious. People variously attributed disease epidemics to the wrath of vengeful gods, or, in a less mystical but equally vague assessment, that they were the result of *miasma*, literally "bad air." Treatment was just as elusive. In the fifth century, the Greek historian Herodotus wrote that in Babylonia the sick were laid out in the street, in the usually vain hope that a passing stranger would know of a cure.

Fundamental misunderstandings about how the world worked were hardly restricted to physicians. Scientists of all descriptions struggled to come to grips with how life itself emerged. The Greek philosopher and natural historian Aristotle made the case so clearly in about 350 BCE that his ideas persisted for two millennia: living things can emerge from nonliving material, like dust or rotting flesh.

In the seventeenth century, a Flemish chemist named Jan Baptiste van Helmont even went so far as to provide simple recipes: to create a mouse, wrap wheat in a piece of soiled cloth and leave it in a cool, dark place for twenty-one days; to create a scorpion, place basil leaves between two bricks and leave them in the sun. The principle that complex living things can only come from other similar living things, called **biogenesis**, would not be firmly settled until 1861.

That does not mean that people in ancient societies were completely ignorant of disease and disease processes. Careful observers had known since biblical times, for example, that disease could be passed from one person to another and also through shared items like utensils or clothing. The Bible itself, in the Book of Leviticus, details how to separate people with skin diseases from the healthy population.

TREATMENTS and TRADITIONS

The fact that the underlying cause of disease remained mysterious did not keep innovative cultures from finding solutions with whatever they had on hand, which usually meant plants or even soil. A three-thousand-year-old tablet from Mesopotamia lists fifteen medicines, many made from plants. Traditional Chinese medicine has for centuries relied on a group of plants and shrubs known by the scientific name *Artemisia*, including species that go by English names like mugwort, wormwood, and sagebrush. Chinese herbalists used these plants to treat a variety of illnesses for thousands of years, but it was only in the 1970s that scientists found one plant that seemed particularly effective in treating malaria. Called sweet wormwood, it is a member of the daisy family, looks a bit like chamomile, and, it turns out, is exceptionally rich in a substance called artemisinin. Extracted from the plants, artemisinin is now among the most effective treatments available for malaria, and the scientist who made the discovery won the Nobel Prize for Medicine in 2015.

Traces of antibiotics have been found in human skeletal remains from ancient Sudan that are more than 2,300 years old, as well as skeletons from an Egyptian oasis that are nearly as old. Scientists believe that antibiotics were present in the diets of these civilizations and that they provided some protection, as evidence suggests that the rate of infection among these groups of people was quite low. In Jordan, people have long rubbed the local red soil on skin infections. It turns out that this soil contains bacteria that produce effective antibiotics.

Between 50 and 70 CE, a Greek surgeon named Dioscorides learned how to make a variety of medicines, including soothing balms and anesthetics from hundreds of plants. He compiled his findings in a book that would come to be called *De Materia Medica*, and it would remain a standard reference for the next 1,500 years.

Traditional, plant-based medicines could be effective, and they remain a standard practice in many parts of the world today. But they did little to prevent epidemics of devastating diseases from sweeping across large swaths of the world. Scarlet fever, typhoid fever, cholera, and most famous of all, bubonic plaque could wipe out cities and bring entire civilizations to their knees. Early physicians could do little but offer some small bit of comfort to the ill and the dying.

ANIMALCULES

The tide began to turn ever so slowly in the favor of humanity in the late seventeenth century. The first hint of progress came from an unlikely source. Antonie van Leeuwenhoek was not a physician, scientist, or scholar. He had little formal education at all; by the age of sixteen he was an apprentice bookkeeper in a shop that sold linen and drapery. But he was soon running his own shop in his hometown of Delft, not far from Amsterdam.

Leeuwenhoek wanted to get a closer look at the quality of thread in the cloth he sold, but he was not satisfied with the quality of the readily available magnifying glasses. He developed an interest in making glass lenses and in a relatively new scientific instrument, the microscope. He built several with different designs, and he soon expanded his interest from simply examining threads and began to look at other things as well, like common mold or the eye of a bee.

This alone was not new. Other scientists, notably the English surveyor, architect, and physicist Robert Hooke, had also used microscopes to examine flies, feathers, snowflakes, and, in particular, cork. Hooke coined the term "cell" to describe the ordered structure of cork that he saw through his microscope.

Antonie van Leeuwenhoek (1623–1723), a Dutch tradesman, built improved microscopes and became the world's first microbiologist.

Like Hooke and others, Leeuwenhoek began his investigation by using his instrument to get a closer look at things he could already see with the naked eye. But then he had an insight that was revolutionary: seemingly simple things like a drop of water, for example, contained things that only the microscope could reveal. When Leeuwenhoek peered through his instrument at a drop of rain he suddenly found an entirely new world. The water, he discovered, was teeming with what he called "animalcules," little creatures with tiny "legs" and "tails." A bit later he found even tinier animals in water that had been infused with ground pepper. When Leeuwenhoek examined his own saliva, he was shocked to discover that he shared his own body with other living things.

The first of Leeuwenhoek's animalcules were what we now call protozoa; the second were almost certainly the first bacteria ever seen by human eyes. Among the creatures he described were some that produced a sort of gas; we know them now as yeasts, the foundation of both bread and wine. Leeuwenhoek's first reports of his discoveries were met with disbelief among the scientific community in Europe. As a tradesman who spoke no language other than his native Dutch—certainly not Latin, the standard language for most scientific communication of his day—he was easy to ignore. Following his death in 1723, Leeuwenhoek and his tiny animals were promptly forgotten.

The true importance of Leeuwenhoek's work would not become clear for over two centuries. Yet great advances were possible even without knowing anything about the microscopic world.

The DISCOVERY of VACCINES

Lady Mary Wortley Montagu came from the noblest of English families. Her father, the first Duke of Kingston-upon-Hull, served as a counselor to King George I and was among the leading figures in high society. Her beauty was so renowned that England's most celebrated painter sought her out, and the resulting portrait inspired England's leading poet, Alexander Pope.

Lady Montagu was far from just a noble with a pretty face. She was also brilliant and decades, if not centuries, ahead of her time. She taught herself Latin, at that time a language reserved for men, and by the age of fifteen had written hundreds of poems and a novel. She married at age twenty-three and joined her husband, a diplomat, in Istanbul. Her writings about life in Turkey would inspire generations of women travelers and writers.

Lady Montagu's life was not all storybook romance and adventure, and that would turn out to be vitally important for posterity. She contracted smallpox in 1715. It was a horrific malady. A seemingly healthy person would suddenly develop a high fever, headache, and backache. She would start to vomit and become delirious. By the third or fourth day of such suffering things would get even worse, as red spots would appear on the face and around the eyes, and these would soon turn to pus-filled blisters.

Smallpox killed 20 to 40 percent of its victims. Even if the patient survived, the blisters would leave permanent, disfiguring scars and even blindness. In the seventeenth and eighteenth centuries, one-third of the population of London bore smallpox scars, Lady Montagu among them.

Smallpox had plagued humanity for millennia. Some scientists believe it emerged more than three thousand years ago in the Indus River valley, at the time the home to the largest civilization on the planet, and was so lethal it effectively wiped out the human population. With no humans to carry the disease and infect others, smallpox itself disappeared, only to reemerge in China in the fourth century CE and in the Mediterranean some three centuries later.

Healers in both China and India searched for cures. They knew that people who survived the disease became immune

Bacteria, Molds, and Viruses

With his relatively crude instruments, Antonie van Leeuwenhoek was just able to make out some tiny, single-celled organisms, far smaller than his "animalcules." Further investigation of these entirely unknown forms of life would await the development of improved microscopes with multiple lenses. (Leeuwenhoek's had one powerful lens, and multi-lens microscopes would not be available until long after Leeuwenhoek's death.)

In 1828, Christian Gottfried Ehrenberg, a German zoologist, used one of the improved microscopes to examine some single-celled, rod-shaped organisms. Their shape led Ehrenberg to name them "bacteria," from the Greek for "stick" or "staff."

Two other microbes are key to the antibiotic story, and they are distinct from bacteria. The first are molds, like the yeast that fascinated both Leeuwenhoek and Louis Pasteur. Yeasts and their relatives are not at all related to bacteria. They are, in fact, an entirely distinct domain of life. Unlike bacteria, which are single celled and have no cell nucleus, fungi (as well as all animals) are multicellular, and those cells have nuclei.

A second microbe is vastly different again from the other two. Viruses are far smaller than any bacteria, too small to be seen by any optical microscope. They can infect all life forms, including bacteria, plants, and animals, and they cause a host of diseases in humans, from the inconvenient common cold to deadly Ebola. Unlike bacterial infections, viruses do not respond to treatment with antibiotics.

Lady Mary Wortley Montagu (1689–1762) campaigned for variolation in England, an early form of vaccination against smallpox.

to further infection, at least for a time. They came up with the idea of provoking a mild case of smallpox by taking a scab from a survivor and grinding it into a fine powder that they then blew into the nose of a healthy person. Arab physicians, meanwhile, had a different method: they made small incisions in a healthy person's arm and rubbed material gleaned from a smallpox blister into them. Whatever the method, the subject in most cases developed a mild case of smallpox and became immune to the disease.

Several people, including an English trader and a Turkish doctor named Emmanuel Timoni, saw the procedures and tried to generate interest in them in England. They failed.

Dr. Timoni returned to his practice in Istanbul where, in 1717, he was asked to assist in the birth of Lady Montagu's second child, a daughter. Seeing her smallpox scars, Timoni asked Lady Montagu to allow him to immunize her firstborn, a son. She agreed, and when she returned home shortly thereafter Lady Montagu and her English physician, Charles Maitland, set about making the procedure widely known. She invited newspaper reporters to witness what was then called **variolation**, from the Latin word for smallpox, *variola*, and convinced the royalty of the need to variolate their own children.

By 1735, some 850 people in Britain had been variolated. It was effective but far from perfect: more than 10 percent of those treated died. While lower than the mortality from the disease itself, such a high rate of complications meant that widespread acceptance of variolation was slow in coming, despite the enthusiastic endorsement of the Royal College of Physicians. A better, safer technique was needed.

Edward Jenner

In the meantime, smallpox remained a deadly scourge. In 1757, an epidemic of the disease struck Britain, and all schoolchildren who had not been variolated were required to do so. Among them was an eight-year-old orphan named Edward Jenner. Yet the procedure was not a simple injection, as we know it today. Physicians of the time had decided, for no apparent reason, that prior to variolation they needed to put their subjects through six weeks of preparation, during which they bled them repeatedly, restricted how much food they could eat, and purged them. Not surprisingly, at the end of this trial the children were weak and miserable. In Jenner's case, to make matter worse, after he received the inoculation he was confined in a room with other children who had the disease and were in many cases deathly ill.

The experience left a lasting impression and may have played a part in Jenner's determination, at the age of just thirteen, to take on an apprenticeship with a country surgeon. Among the stories he heard during his six years of training was that milkmaids who caught cowpox—a harmless disease that affected the udders and teats of cows—on their hands never developed smallpox later. Jenner filed that idea away in his brain. It would remain a topic of interest thereafter, but it would be nearly thirty years before he returned to it in full.

In 1796, having experimented with swinepox, a related disease of pigs, Jenner finally returned to the idea that he could take pus from a cowpox lesion, inject it into a healthy person, and thereby make that person immune to smallpox. At the time, the idea of experimenting on human beings was not regarded with the same horror that it is today. Jenner selected for his test an eight-year-old boy named James Phipps, son of a homeless laborer.

Jenner made two small incisions on the boy's arm. He dipped his lancet first into the cowpox lesions on the hands of local girl Sarah Nelmes, then into the incisions. After eight days, James developed pustules similar to cowpox and a slight fever, but both soon faded. A month after the initial procedure,

Jenner variolated James, which should have produced a mild case of smallpox. Yet no such symptoms appeared. Jenner had for the first time demonstrated that giving a healthy person a mild disease could protect him or her against a far more devastating one. In the process, he developed a safe way to eradicate smallpox. That task would not be complete until 1980, and smallpox remains the only infectious disease that medical science has completely destroyed.

Jenner referred to his method by the awkward but descriptive phrase "cowpox inoculation." It would be several years before another physician, Richard Dunning, coined a more pleasing alternative. The Latin for "cowpox" is *vaccinia*, so Dunning, and soon most everyone else, called Jenner's method "vaccination."

LOUIS PASTEUR and the BIRTH of MICROBIOLOGY

In 1856, a French winemaker, troubled by a product that turned sour after long storage, sought the advice of a local chemist named Louis Pasteur. During these studies, Pasteur determined that both beer and wine were essentially the products of some of the yeasts that Leeuwenhoek had described, though it is doubtful Pasteur had ever heard of the Dutchman's research.

Pasteur did far more than determine the role that yeasts play in fermentation. He also realized that the problems the winemaker and his colleagues were having stemmed from stray yeasts in the air finding their way into containers of beer and wine and spoiling them. Then Pasteur took another step: he found that gently heating fluids destroys contaminating yeasts and bacteria. Pasteur saved France's wine industry and while

In 1796, Edward Jenner (1749–1823) performed the first smallpox vaccination on eight-year-old James Phipps. The boy survived, and smallpox was finally eliminated in 1980.

Heating food and drink, like the milk in this processing plant, to kill bacteria is called pasteurization and is used around the world to make food safe to eat.

doing so invented the process, now called pasteurization, that is a fundamental tool for food preservation worldwide.

Having saved one industry, Pasteur was next called on to save another. Silk production was one of the main ways that people in rural France earned a living. But silkworms were dying in droves across the country. Pasteur knew nothing about making silk, but he suspected that microorganisms were again the culprits. Though he never found the precise germ, he was able to devise ways of identifying the disease early and keep it from spreading. A savior again, Pasteur soon rose to prominence as the most famous scientist in Europe, if not the world.

Antiseptics and the Germ Theory of Disease

Pasteur was beginning, slowly and steadily, to accumulate the evidence for the vital role that microorganisms play in the world around us. Through he was not a physician, and never treated humans, he also began to realize that just as microbes can take hold in vats of wine or trays full of silkworms, so too can they occupy the human body.

Discoveries over the next decade or so gave both medicine and the science of microorganisms an enormous boost. First, in 1865, an English surgeon named Joseph Lister read Pasteur's studies on the role of yeast in souring wine. Lister was all too familiar with the problem that many patients in his and other hospitals survived their operations but succumbed soon after to what was then known as "ward fever." After reading Pasteur, Lister had an insight that would transform medical practice: the process that caused a wound to fester, or "suppurate," was not all that different from fermentation. Perhaps it was airborne microbes settling into open wounds that were causing the problem.

Lister decided to apply dressings soaked in carbolic acid to post-operative wounds. He also introduced the idea of

Louis Pasteur (1822–1895) made a series of important breakthroughs in the study of disease, particularly providing direct support for the idea that germs cause diseases like anthrax and rabies.

"**antiseptic**" surgery: using carbolic acid and other techniques to ensure that any germs present in an operating room were killed. Lister was able to reduce deaths in his hospital but faced persistent opposition from medical authorities of the day, who remained convinced that there was nothing to be done to prevent suppuration. Part of the problem was that Lister believed, but could not prove, that microbes in the air existed and could cause disease in humans. When that proof came, it would be the next great leap for science.

In 1876, an obscure and unassuming German physician and microbiologist named Robert Koch proved that a bacterium called ***Bacillus*** *anthracis* caused the disease anthrax in humans. Working with handmade tools in a curtained-off corner of his examination room, Koch was able to isolate the bacillus from sick animals, **culture** it, and inject it into guinea pigs and other animals. It was the first time that a disease had been conclusively linked to a germ, an absolutely vital step in the development of modern medicine.

For one thing, Koch provided a firm scientific foundation for the idea of antiseptics. While Lister continued to face opposition and even ridicule, he honed his surgical techniques and the antiseptics he used, and with other physicians promoted the idea of cleaning surgical instrument, patients' skin, and doctors' hands. All these steps are second nature today, but they were revolutionary at the time.

Robert Koch's discovery of anthrax had other impacts as well. Not long after news of that discovery reached France, Louis Pasteur took the first of what would be two momentous vacations in the history of science (Alexander Fleming's would be the second, half a century later). Pasteur was working on the disease of cholera in chickens, and one day he accidently injected two of his flock with a culture that was several weeks old. The chickens sickened but did not die. Then, he and his entire laboratory staff went on holiday. When they returned, they set about to inject chickens with a fresh batch of cholera. As expected, the chickens all died, except for the two that had survived the older batch.

Pasteur knew instantly that he had made a great discovery, perhaps the most important of his already dazzling career: injection of an old culture of cholera germs afforded protection against a far more virulent form of the disease. The same thing could be true for other germs and other diseases, like anthrax. After much trial and error, Pasteur devised a method to weaken (or attenuate) the anthrax bacillus that Koch has discovered. A giant public demonstration was planned.

On May 5, 1881, on a farm southeast of Paris, Pasteur and his assistants injected twenty-four of forty-eight sheep, three of six cows, and one of two goats with the attenuated anthrax. He waited three weeks then injected all of the animals with a deadly dose of live bacteria. The next day, Pasteur arrived at the farm to a cheering crowd, and he knew the demonstration had been a success. All the untreated sheep were dead or dying, while those who had received the vaccine were grazing happily in a field. The same was true of the cows and the goats as well. At long last, more than eighty years after Edward Jenner's successful vaccinations against smallpox, science had revealed how the process worked, and most important, how it could be repeated.

Pasteur, triumphant, was a hero of France yet again. But still he was not finished. Four years later, Pasteur developed a vaccine for rabies. By this time his fame had spread to America and Europe's most remote corners. A rabid wolf had terrorized a Russian village, and a group of peasants arrived in France able to utter but a single word: Pasteur. He treated them over the course of a week, with all of Paris following the story.

When sixteen of the peasants survived and returned to Russia, Tsar Alexander III was so grateful he donated a large sum of money to help create the Pasteur Institute, which remains one of the world's leading centers for research on microorganisms, disease, and vaccines.

Louis Pasteur died in 1895, but he lived long enough to see even more progress, such as the identification of the organisms that cause diphtheria and plague. He did not live to see the full impact of the discoveries he had made, which would continue to play out for decades, as more and more vaccines were developed and a way to combat bacterial infections finally emerged.

The penicillin mold (*Penicillium notatum*) was first described in 1809 and was of interest to scientists long before Alexander Fleming.

CHAPTER 2

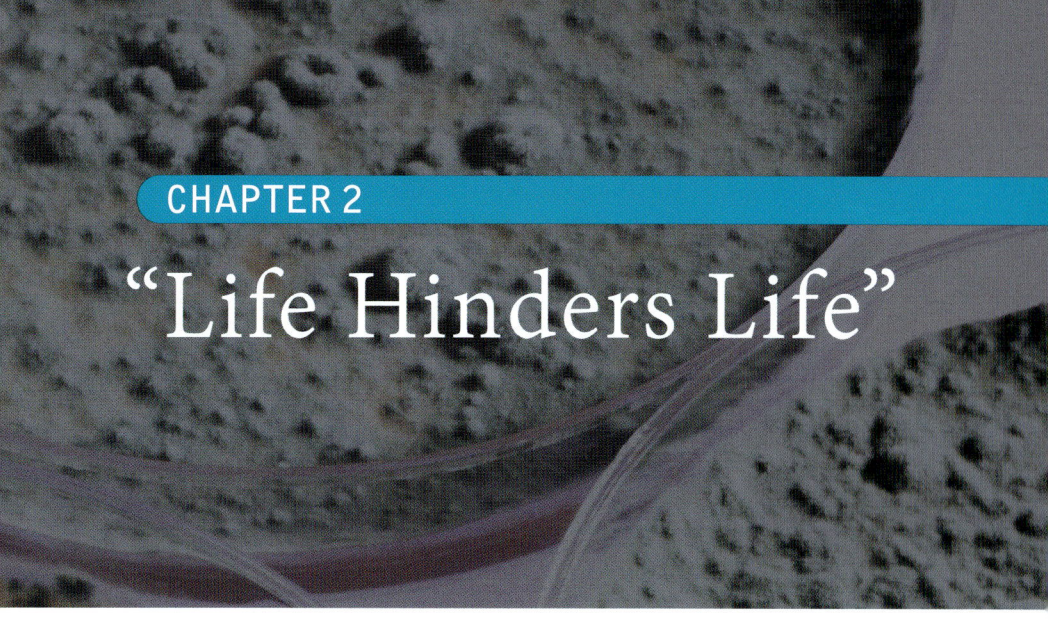

"Life Hinders Life"

Scientists like Jenner, Pasteur, Koch, and Lister laid the groundwork for the discovery of antibiotics. Yet much more work remained to be done. One piece of the puzzle had actually been filled in, though it would be some time before anyone realized that fact. In 1875, John Tyndall was already one of England's most distinguished scientists. He had, among other things, proved the existence of a greenhouse effect in Earth's atmosphere (a key part of the modern study of climate change) and made important contributions to delineating the separation of science and religion, and he was a champion of Charles Darwin and his theory of evolution.

Tyndall had been most interested in physics and questions of heat, light, and sound. His studies of light, however, were hindered by dust in the air, so he began looking for a way to clean it and create what he called "optically pure" air. In so doing he stumbled almost accidentally into the world of microbiology.

JOHN TYNDALL and MICROBIOLOGY

Tyndall built a square, wooden box with glass windows and coated the inside walls and floor of the box with sticky glycerin. After three days, he directed a strong beam of light through the windows and found that there were no particles in the air; all the dust had gotten stuck in the glycerin. By this time, Tyndall had read Pasteur's work and had become a great admirer. The two began a lengthy correspondence, and Tyndall realized that not only was the air in his Tyndall Box optically pure, it was in fact completely germ free.

To prove this point, Tyndall boiled meat broth then put some samples in the clean air of the Tyndall Box and left others outside of it. After just a few days, the test tubes outside the box grew cloudy and putrid, while those inside it remained clear and "sweet"—as Tyndall put it—for months. Tyndall then decided to seek out answers to a separate but related question: bacteria were clearly distributed in the air, but were they distributed evenly? That is, were you as likely to encounter bacteria in one place as another, or were bacteria clumped together, like clouds in the sky?

Tyndall believed bacteria were evenly distributed, and he set up an experiment to prove it. He took one hundred test tubes containing broth and distributed them about his laboratory. The next day, Tyndall examined the tubes and found that some were cloudy, but others were clear. Bacteria had invaded some of the test tubes but not others, and thus bacteria were not evenly distributed.

While Tyndall's hypothesis about the distribution of bacteria was wrong, he was right in believing that bacteria are everywhere. They are on surfaces, in the air, in water, and most of all, in us. Our bodies host thousands upon thousands of species of bacteria, and scientists are just beginning to understand the full extent of the complex roles they play not just in disease but in keeping us healthy as well. Given the multiple communities of bacteria in our mouths, intestines, and blood vessels, and on our skin, it is not a stretch to say that without bacteria, we would not be human.

Had Tyndall stopped his investigation by disproving his own hypothesis the matter might have ended there, with a new but not earth-shattering addition to the still-young science of bacteriology. But then things got quite a bit more interesting and important. After another twenty-four hours, Tyndall noticed mold growing on the surface of the broth in some of the tubes. He described it as "exquisitely beautiful," blue-green with distinctive brush-shaped structures that gave the mold its name: *Penicillium notatum*; in Latin, a *penicillius* is an artist's fine brush made of camel hair.

Penicillium is a common mold, found on food and in damp places around a house or a lab. Scientists before Tyndall had noticed some interesting characteristics as well, beyond its pleasing color. In 1870, an English scientist named Sir John Scott Burdon-Sanderson observed that a culture fluid covered with the mold would not grow bacteria. The following year, Joseph Lister also found that urine samples contaminated with *Penicillium* did not grow bacteria.

Tyndall was more systematic. He described a battle between the mold and the bacteria:

> In every case where the mold was thick and coherent the bacteria died, or became dormant, and fell to the bottom as sediment. The growth of the mold and its effects on the bacteria was very capricious … The bacteria which manufacture a green pigment appear to be uniformly victorious in their fight with the *Penicillium*.

Just a year later, Louis Pasteur began to see the bigger picture. Perhaps physicians could harness this kind of microbial warfare to fight disease, writing:

> In the inferior and vegetable species, still more than in the big animal and vegetable species, life hinders life. A liquid invaded by an organized ferment, or by an aerobe, makes it difficult for an inferior organism to multiply … These facts may, perhaps, justify the greatest hope from the therapeutic point of view.

"Life hinders life" would become one of Pasteur's most famous pronouncements. It is a parallel to his idea of biogenesis, which essentially means "all life from life." The idea of using one type of living thing to combat another type that is detrimental to human health would form a key building block of modern medicine.

Yet while Tyndall had shown that something about *Penicillium* enabled it to destroy bacteria, he did not know what, and not even a towering figure like Louis Pasteur was able to make the final leap. The relationship between bacteria and human disease was becoming clearer by the day, but the true, overwhelming significance of the work by Tyndall and Pasteur was hidden and would remain so for decades.

IMMUNOLOGY

Despite the fact that Koch and Pasteur conclusively demonstrated the germ theory of disease not long after Tyndall had shown the effectiveness of *Penicillium* in killing bacteria, no one made the connection. It was not as if research into the question stopped altogether. In 1889, a French mycologist (a scientist who studies fungi) named Jean-Paul Vuillemin observed how fungi and yeasts can destroy bacteria, and he coined a new word to describe the fight for survival between two organisms: "antibiosis," literally meaning "against life."

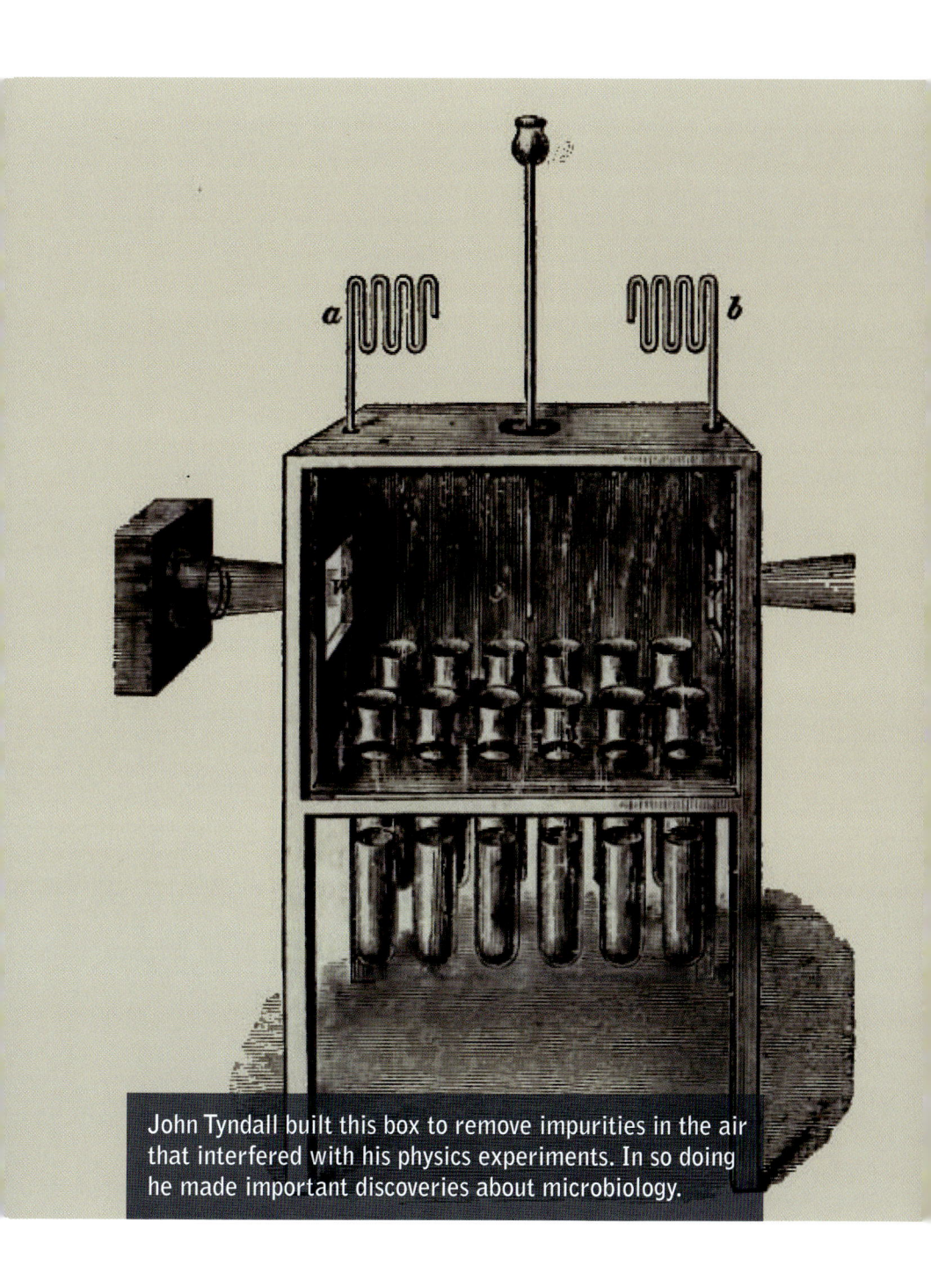

John Tyndall built this box to remove impurities in the air that interfered with his physics experiments. In so doing he made important discoveries about microbiology.

"Life Hinders Life" 33

The idea that physicians could fight infections with chemicals that had been developed in a lab was still years off. Most medical scientists rejected it. In part that was due to Pasteur's spectacular success in demonstrating the effectiveness of vaccines. For Pasteur and for medical science in general for the next seventy years, the way to fight bacteria was to mobilize the body's own defenses against them. The specialty that emerged out of the study of that approach would come to be called immunology.

In the early years, when physicians were making great strides in combating diseases like the plague, anthrax, and yellow fever, they had no real idea why their vaccines were working. The modern understanding that white blood cells called lymphocytes recognize foreign cells like bacteria and mobilize a host of defenses to kill them emerged only in the mid-twentieth century and was the product of hundreds of scientists, a number of whom won Nobel Prizes for their work.

Yet even without any understanding of the process, scientists in the late nineteenth century made tremendous progress, developing a host of vaccines and successfully immunizing thousands of people against infection. It should thus come as no surprise that the overwhelming emphasis of physicians as they entered a new century was to find more ways to work with the body's own systems.

Many scientist also still believed in the principle of vitalism, which held that the laws of chemistry and physics did not explain the processes of life because they could not account for the "vital spark" that separates the living from the nonliving world. The methods that nature had developed must provide the best cures, according to the reasoning at the time. That idea was so powerful that it closed off other avenues of research and delayed the discovery of antibiotics for years.

The MAGIC BULLET

In the mid-nineteenth century, German industry faced a problem. Unlike England and France, Germany had few colonies overseas and thus had less access to various raw materials. Among the things Germany lacked were the plants and minerals used to make natural dyes for textiles. In order to compete, German companies needed to figure out how to make artificial dyes from chemicals.

They succeeded beyond their wildest dreams, and by the end of the century nearly all new chemical dyes were coming from German companies. The research brought a host of other discoveries as well, most importantly the **Haber-Bosch process** for the industrial-scale production of ammonia, which led to fertilizers that revolutionized farming around the world.

The dye industry led down another path as well. Scientists began to play around with dyes and noticed that particular bacteria would pick up the color of one stain, but not another. To this day bacteriologists classify bacteria into two broad categories according to whether they take up a violet dye first used by Danish bacteriologist Hans Christian Gram in 1884. **Gram-positive bacteria** take up the stain and turn violet, while **Gram-negative bacteria** turn pink. The difference is important because it reflects properties of the cell walls; Gram-positive bacteria will take up antibiotics in much the same way as they take up the stain and thus are more susceptible to the drugs. Infections caused by Gram-negative bacteria are far harder to treat and would be a problem for physicians until the 1950s.

A German physician and scientist named Paul Ehrlich was the first to understand the significance of the fact that certain cells and cell structures absorb dyes while others do not. He reasoned that he might be able to find a chemical that would be taken up by and then kill only a specific kind of cell, say a bacteria, and leave the surrounding cells untouched. That would allow physicians to cure disease without harming their patients. He called his as-yet undiscovered substance a "magic bullet," and he called the therapeutic method he invented "chemotherapy."

Ehrlich began his search with a compound of arsenic called **atoxyl**. He knew it was highly toxic to a certain class of bacteria, called **spirochetes** because of their spiral shape. Spirochetes cause a variety of diseases in humans, including Lyme disease and **leptospirosis**. Most important from Ehrlich's perspective, however, was a spirochete known as *Treponema palladium,* which causes syphilis.

Treating the Scourge

Syphilis was widespread and almost incurable in Europe, and it had been a problem for centuries. It took hold after King Charles VIII of France invaded Naples in 1495 with fifty thousand soldiers, mostly mercenaries from across Europe, who on their return spread the disease to their home countries. It was called "the great pox" (smallpox was named to distinguish it from syphilis), and by the early sixteenth century it was already a scourge.

Syphilis can linger in the body for years, leading eventually to seizures, dementia, and death. In 1520, the Dutch scholar and theologian Erasmus said: "If I were asked which is the most destructive of all diseases I should unhesitatingly reply, it is that which for some years has been raging with impunity … What contagion does thus invade the whole body, so much resist medical art, becomes inoculated so readily, and so cruelly tortures the patient?"

Treatment for syphilis involved mercury, either as an ointment rubbed into the skin or inhaled as fumes, or both. That treatment could last for years. While mercury is a poison and could indeed kill the organism that causes syphilis, at least as often it killed the patient as well.

Once physicians realized that the side effects of mercury far outweighed the benefits, they began to search for alternatives, which at various times included sarsaparilla root, iodine, platinum, and gold. None were effective.

Scientists finally identified the bacterium that causes syphilis in 1905. Paul Ehrlich found that arsenic was extremely effective in killing the syphilis spirochete, but, like mercury, it was too toxic. Ehrlich believed that some modified version of atoxyl could be the magic bullet. He began a laborious, systematic effort to find it. One by one, he and his team produced atoxyl derivatives and tested them on rabbits that had been infected with the disease.

Finally, in 1909, after testing 605 different compounds, they found one that cured the disease and did not kill the rabbits. First called Compound 606 and later sold under the name **Salvarsan**, the drug was the first to show even modest success against syphilis in humans.

Salvarsan also marked the first time modern science had created a substance in the laboratory that could be safely injected into people and destroy a particular microorganism. (Quinine, derived from bark of the South American cinchona tree, had been used for centuries to treat malaria.) The painstaking method Ehrlich introduced is still the basis for nearly all efforts to develop new drugs.

Fighting Streptococcus

The combination of systematic testing and an interest in dyes would also lead to the next step in antibiotics. A pathologist working for the German pharmaceutical company Bayer found that an orange-red dye called sulfamidochrysodine protected mice from infection with a streptococcus bacteria, the cause of strep throat and a host of other illnesses in humans. One of the most serious illness streptococci can cause is called puerperal fever, which attacks new mothers and is often fatal. The drug Bayer found, eventually sold as **Prontosil**, was remarkably effective against puerperal fever, and that led to the discovery of an entire class of medications called sulfonamides, or sulfa drugs.

Sulfa drugs were less effective against syphilis than Salvarsan, which remained a common treatment for syphilis until the 1940s. Scientists still do not know exactly how Salvarsan worked, more than one hundred years after it was discovered, and a lingering controversy about its chemical structure was only resolved in 2005.

Salvarsan saved lives and relieved suffering, but it was far from perfect. Like mercury it is toxic, too toxic to administer more than once a week—it can cause kidney failure, seizures, fever, and rash, among other things. Salvarsan was difficult to use as well. The powdered form of the drug needed to be diluted in more than two cups of water, and that large quantity of fluid all had to be injected directly into the vein of the patient through the broad needles available at the time. If any of the mixture escaped the vein it could kill the surrounding tissue, and sometimes doctors would have to amputate the arm to prevent further damage or even death.

Ehrlich delivered some samples of Salvarsan to a friend and colleague named Almroth Wright, a prominent scientist in London. Wright, however, was one of the leading opponents of the very idea of chemotherapy. Another scientist who worked in Wright's lab shared this skepticism: Alexander Fleming.

Sir Almroth Wright (1861–1947) directed the Inoculation Department at St. Mary's Hospital, London. He worked closely with Alexander Fleming but was skeptical of antibiotics.

Paul Ehrlich

Paul Ehrlich was born on March 14, 1854, in Strehlen in Silesia, in what is now southwest Poland. As a medical student, Ehrlich found that different chemical dyes stained cells depending on their type, which led Ehrlich to the groundbreaking idea that chemical agents could help heal cells because of the way that the dye was taken in to the cell during cellular processes.

Ehrlich developed a new staining technique to identify the bacterium that causes tuberculosis. His work identifying blood cells led to an entirely new field, hematology. But Ehrlich contracted tuberculosis as a result of his work, and he traveled to Egypt in search of a cure.

When Ehrlich returned to Germany he became interested in the questions of how bacteria bring about disease. Ehrlich's new understanding of immunity was crucial to many advances in immunology as well as in the development of an effective treatment for diphtheria. He was awarded the Nobel Prize in Medicine in 1908 for his immunity research.

Paul Ehrlich died of stroke in August 1915. In his obituary, the *London Times* wrote, "The whole world is in his debt."

German physician and scientist Paul Ehrlich (1854–1915) made important discoveries in hematology, immunology, and chemotherapy. He won the Nobel Prize in 1908.

ALMROTH WRIGHT

Almroth Wright was one of the most colorful and controversial scientists in England. He was arrogant, domineering yet charming, and prone to lengthy and public battles with anyone who disagreed with him. He was also, without doubt, brilliant.

In 1898, Wright developed a vaccine against typhoid fever, which at the time was almost always fatal and was a particular problem for armies during wartime. The army rejected his ideas during the Second Boer War in South Africa (1899–1902), and thousands of soldiers died from preventable disease.

Wright, however, was nothing if not persistent. He became a professor of bacteriology at St. Mary's Hospital in London and turned his laboratory in the Inoculation Department into a vaccine factory. He helped produce millions of doses of typhoid vaccine, and during World War I, Wright convinced the army to use it, thus saving the lives of as many as half a million soldiers. Britain was the only combatant to immunize its troops against typhoid, and for the first time fewer British soldiers died from infection than from wounds. Wright's vaccine is essentially the same one in use today.

Wright summed up his approach like this: the only way to treat disease is to "mobilize the immunological garrison." That became his motto, and it dominated the work of one of England's most prestigious research labs. Building on the work of scientists from Pasteur onward, he believed that while drugs could temporarily alleviate symptoms of diseases, only the body's natural defenses could bring about a cure.

Wright made another major contribution that would play a key role in the development of antibiotics, almost in spite of himself. Wright was a firm believer in the scientific method of hypothesis and experimentation, and he tended

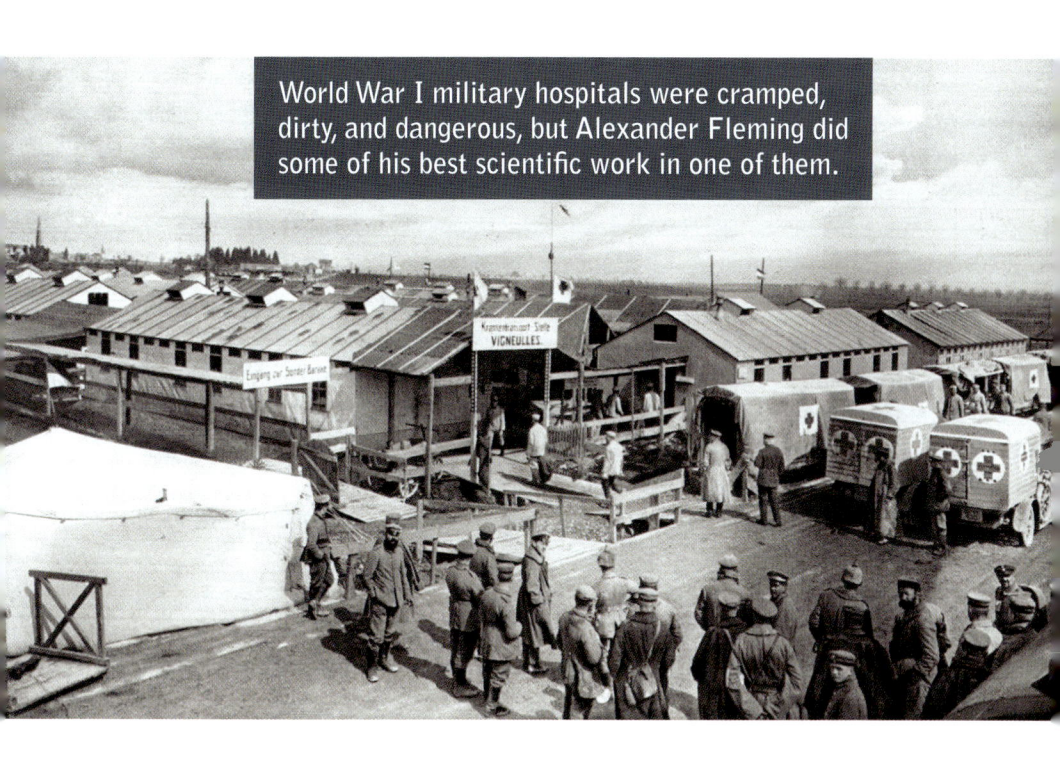

World War I military hospitals were cramped, dirty, and dangerous, but Alexander Fleming did some of his best scientific work in one of them.

"Life Hinders Life" 43

to distrust the day-to-day clinical experience of physicians as insufficiently rigorous. During World War I, military surgeons treating battle wounds followed Joseph Lister's advice and used an antiseptic solution of carbolic acid. Wright thought this was misguided.

Wright had by this time been joined in the Inoculation Department by a brilliant but unassuming researcher from Scotland named Alexander Fleming. The conditions they faced during the war could hardly have been more daunting. Stationed in France at an old casino that had been turned into a hospital, they set up cleaning stations designed to handle two hundred wounded soldiers a day. By 1914, they had to treat more than a thousand soldiers every day; with so little space, some of the wounded had to lie on the battlefield for a day or more awaiting treatment.

The standard treatment was not to close up the wounds but to pack them with bandages soaked in carbolic acid. The reasoning behind that approach seemed sound enough: Joseph Lister had shown that chemicals killed bacteria on the surface of the skin and on surgical instruments, so it made sense to believe they would also kill bacteria once infection had set into a wound. But they did not, and infection was rampant in the makeshift hospital.

Together, Wright and Fleming showed that while antiseptics killed harmful bacteria, they were even more effective at killing beneficial blood cells called macrophages and neutrophils that gathered in wounds and are crucial to the healing process. In other words, using antiseptics on wounds that were already infected made things worse instead of better. Wright and Fleming also found that the antiseptic paste commonly used to coat wounds encouraged the growth of bacteria that can grow in the absence of oxygen. These so-called **anaerobes** are responsible for deadly diseases that cause terrible suffering and death during war: tetanus and gangrene.

Wright and Fleming developed a new approach: cut away as much of the damaged tissues as possible, clean the wound with sterile saline solution, and close it up with sutures often made of sterile catgut. That helped, but not much. Infection continued to kill soldiers by the score.

That wartime experience deepened Wright's and Fleming's skepticism about using drugs to treat infections inside the body, as opposed to on the surface. Both of them, along with many others, considered **antibacterial** drugs a delusion. Nevertheless, when Wright passed on Paul Ehrlich's sample of Salvarsan, Fleming eagerly accepted it.

Fleming had trained as a surgeon (though he never performed an operation) and his skilled hands could manipulate the crude syringes and needles better than most of his colleagues. He became a sought-after physician for the treatment of syphilis, a lucrative practice that eventually enabled him to buy an opulent London apartment as well as a large country house, unheard-of luxuries for most laboratory scientists of the day.

The contradiction between Fleming's distrust of chemotherapy and his use of it to treat his patients would in important ways shape his response to the accidental discovery he would later make.

The LYSOZYME

While Fleming's syphilis practice flourished—he treated prominent artists who often paid him with paintings and thus amassed an impressive collection—his research continued in almost the opposite direction. Expanding on his work from the war, Fleming continued to look for antibacterial substances, but for external rather than internal use. In 1921, Fleming found what he was looking for, quite literally right under his own nose.

Fleming had a head cold that fall, and being a curious, even playful scientist, he took some of the mucus from his runny nose and placed it in a petri dish—a shallow, lidded glass dish used to grow bacteria. When he picked up the dish again a week or so later he looked at it closely for a long time and then handed it to one of his assistants.

"This is interesting," was all he said. Fleming was a man of few words, even in the face of something dramatic. Fleming saw that there were yellow colonies of bacteria on the dish but also large areas where there was no growth and other areas where some bacteria had become translucent and glassy and seemed to be dissolving.

Fleming isolated the substance that was dissolving the bacteria and found that it existed not only in mucus but also in saliva, tears, breast milk, egg whites, turnips, and other animal and vegetable material. He decided that the substance might play a role in protecting the body from airborne bacteria, since it turned up in the places bacteria might invade, like the mouth, nose, and eyes.

Almroth Wright eventually gave the substance a name: **lysozyme**, from *lysis*, the Greek for "loosening" and indicating decomposition, and *enzyme*, a biological molecule that speeds up reactions. Lysozyme was powerful, and Fleming hoped that it would turn out to be an antibacterial, but he would be disappointed. The kinds of bacteria that lysozyme dissolves do not infect humans. Bacteria that cause common illnesses, like streptococcus, staphylococcus (which can cause food poisoning, sinus infections, and a host of other diseases), diphtheria, and anthrax are immune to its effects.

While lysozyme was an ineffective antibacterial, that did not prevent Fleming from spending much of his career pursuing it. It also quite likely provided him further evidence that chemotherapy would never work as a treatment for human illness. The reaction of the scientific community played a part as well. When Fleming presented his work on lysozyme to the prestigious Medical Research Club in London, he was met with stony silence. No one seemed to think this was an avenue worth pursuing. The next time Alexander Fleming found something unexpected in his petri dish, he would be more cautious, and yet he would be met with almost the exact same response. The history of medicine, and potentially the lives of million of people, would have been quite a bit different had Fleming been able to transform that silence into enthusiasm, but it was not in his character to do so. The real miracle work would be left to others.

Alexander Fleming in his laboratory at St. Mary's Hospital, London. Fleming was untidy, and his lab was a breeding ground for the unexpected.

CHAPTER 3

Major Players in the Discovery of Antibiotics

Alexander Fleming gets most of the credit for the discovery of penicillin and thus the opening of the antibiotic era of medicine. He became during his lifetime one of the most famous and beloved scientists in the world, recipient of a knighthood, numerous honorary degrees, magazine covers, and a Nobel Prize. His fame continued after his death; in 1970, the International Astronomical Union named a crater on the dark side of the moon for him.

The story of the discovery of penicillin is actually more complicated. Fleming was indeed the first scientist to rigorously pursue the antibacterial action of the *Penicillium* mold. But Fleming was unable to isolate the active ingredient, which he named penicillin, and he turned his back on the effort for more than a decade.

The discovery of penicillin was less a flash of insight than a laborious, frustrating, stop-and-go task of solving one complicated problem after another. Fleming was brilliant, but he was not cut out for that kind of work. The task of transforming penicillin from an interesting laboratory phenomenon into a miracle drug that saved millions of lives and changed the world fell instead to a group of dogged, clever researchers at Oxford University, led by Howard Florey, Ernst Boris Chain, and Norman Heatley.

Florey and Chain both achieved some fame for their work—they shared the Nobel Prize with Fleming and eventually were knighted as well. Norman Heatley, on the other hand, has been almost entirely overlooked. While Fleming remains a towering figure in the history of science, almost a household name, Florey, Chain, and Heatley have been largely forgotten.

Yet without the combined talents of all four of these scientists, the world would be a far different place. Henry Harris, a scientist who knew all of them, put it this way in his memoir: "Without Fleming, no Chain or Florey; without Chain, no Florey; without Florey, no Heatley; without Heatley, no penicillin."

ALEXANDER FLEMING

In one of his most famous pronouncements, Louis Pasteur said, "In the fields of observation chance favors only the prepared mind." That serves as a perfect description of Alexander Fleming. His was a fully prepared mind, and he was lucky, too.

Fleming was born on Lochfield Farm near the town of Darvel, Scotland, 25 miles (40 kilometers) south of Glasgow, in 1881. He was the seventh of eight children of a hard-working sheep farmer. Slight of build, and just less than 5 foot 6 inches (1.7 meters) tall, Fleming was a natural athlete, a good shot with a rifle, but also shy and socially awkward. His most notable physical feature was his large, blue eyes, though some people found that he seemed to look through or past whomever he was talking to. He was not overly fond of conversation. One friend said of him, "Talking to him was like playing tennis with a man who, whenever you knocked the ball over to his side, put it in his pocket."

A solid but unexceptional student who relied on his good memory to sail through his early school years, Fleming did not see himself destined for a career in science or medicine. When

Many scientists before Fleming had stumbled upon penicillin. Only he had the insight to explore its possibilities.

several of his older brothers moved to London, Alexander joined them and quickly excelled in school, but when he graduated at sixteen he was dispatched to the world of business rather than science. His job as a clerk for a shipping company was dull, however, and after four years of drudgery—and with an inheritance from an uncle in his pocket—he leapt at an opportunity to take the entrance exams for medical school.

Fleming did well enough on the exams that he had his choice of any of the dozen medical schools in London. He enrolled at St. Mary's Hospital Medical School, the newest of them all, in 1901, partly because it was the closest to his home, and partly because he had been part of a water polo match against the medical students and had admired their camaraderie and team spirit. Whatever the reason, Fleming's choice of St. Mary's would prove to be a momentous one.

In 1905, Fleming passed the exams to become a fellow of the Royal College of Surgeons, a prestigious institution, but he preferred research to surgery. Instead of performing operations, Fleming joined the Inoculation Department at St. Mary's in 1906. His plan was to stay only briefly and then choose his medical specialty. He ended up staying nearly fifty years and became a pioneer in bacteriology.

Under Almroth Wright, the Inoculation Department was unique in British medicine. The department treated private patients and sold vaccines, and thus was independent of both St. Mary's Hospital and the medical school. With that income, plus the generosity of private donors, including a prime minister, the department paid rent and was given a wing of the hospital with research labs and space to treat patients. It was an exciting place to be, full of visitors from far and wide, including notables from British high society and the arts, including the playwright George Bernard Shaw, who included a character based on Wright in his play *The Doctor's Dilemma*.

While St. Mary's was independent and exciting, it was hardly luxurious, with crowded labs often lacking the latest equipment. Fortunately, Fleming was a master of improvisation and mistrusted labs full of fancy gear. When he and Wright went to France during World War I, Fleming said his lab there, stuffed into the attic of the old casino in a war zone, was one of the best he had worked in, and it was the location of what many people still believe to be his best scientific work.

As a scientist, Fleming was curious and playful. He often painted images using bacteria, taking advantage of the fact that different bacteria take on different colors as they grow. He would streak various types of bacteria across the agar—a jelly-like substance made from seaweed that fills the bottom of a petri dish and provides a growth medium for bacteria. Fleming had both a deep understanding of how bacteria grow as well as the artistic imagination to foresee the finished drawing, which would emerge in slow motion over days or weeks.

Fleming could also be untidy, even sloppy. He often left a sink full of unwashed glassware; his lab was a breeding ground for the unexpected, and he was always on the lookout for it. "I play with microbes," Fleming said. "There are, of course many rules to this play ... but when you have acquired knowledge and experience it is very pleasant to break the rules and to be able to find something nobody had thought of."

Fleming was a talented scientist but he lacked one crucial skill: he was not persuasive. He was a serviceable writer but a poor speaker—students largely avoided his lectures because they were boring. One colleague said, "He had an almost pathological inability to communicate." That characteristic meant that Fleming was often unable to arouse in others whatever excitement he may have had in his own discoveries, and it would have a telling impact on the development of antibiotics.

In His Own Words: Alexander Fleming's Nobel Prize Lecture

The following is an excerpt from Alexander Fleming's Nobel Prize lecture, from December 11, 1945:

> I have been frequently asked why I invented the name "Penicillin." I simply followed perfectly orthodox lines and coined a word which explained that the substance penicillin was derived from a plant of the genus *Penicillium* just as many years ago the word "Digitalin" was invented for a substance derived from the plant *Digitalis*. To my generation of bacteriologists the inhibition of one microbe by another was commonplace. We were all taught about these inhibitions and indeed it is seldom that an observant clinical bacteriologist can pass a week without seeing in the course of his ordinary work very definite instances of bacterial antagonism.
>
> It seems likely that this fact that bacterial antagonisms were so common and well-known hindered rather than helped the initiation of the study of antibiotics as we know it today.
>
> Certainly the older work on antagonism had no influence on the beginning of penicillin. It arose simply from a fortunate occurrence

which happened when I was working on a purely academic bacteriological problem which had nothing to do with antagonism, or molds, or antiseptics, or antibiotics.

In my first publication I might have claimed that I had come to the conclusion, as a result of serious study of the literature and deep thought, that valuable antibacterial substances were made by molds and that I set out to investigate the problem. That would have been untrue and I preferred to tell the truth that penicillin started as a chance observation. My only merit is that I did not neglect the observation and that I pursued the subject as a bacteriologist.

HOWARD FLOREY

Howard Walter Florey was a physiologist, a pathologist, a specialist in internal medicine, and an ambitious, fiery, and hard-driving researcher. Though no one realized it at the time, he was exactly the kind of scientist the search for penicillin would need.

Florey was born on September 24, 1898, in Adelaide, Australia. The son of a prosperous bootmaker, he enrolled at the finest schools and excelled in science, particularly physics and chemistry. He studied medicine, but the emphasis in Australia was training practicing physicians rather than researchers, which was Florey's real interest.

In 1922, Florey got his chance to pursue a research career when he won a Rhodes scholarship to deepen his studies of medicine and physiology at Oxford. He was brilliant, hard working, and intense, and he soon came to the attention of professor Charles Sherrington, an expert in the nervous system who later won a Nobel Prize for his work on the functions of neurons—he even coined the word "neurons." Sherrington became a key mentor. He encouraged Florey to study the capillaries in the brain and then to apply for a prized internship at Cambridge, which he won and which effectively launched his career as an experimental scientist.

The scientific community beyond Oxford began to recognize Florey's great potential as well. He won fellowships to study in Philadelphia and Chicago, and he joined an expedition to the Arctic. While he was in Philadelphia, a classmate referred to him affectionately as "a rough colonial genius." When Florey returned to Britain he took up, among other interests, the study of lysozyme, which Fleming had discovered several years earlier. Fleming even provided Florey with bacterial cultures to carry on the work, but it proved inconclusive in proving that lysozyme played an important role in natural immunity.

Florey's big break came in 1935, when he was appointed chair of pathology at the William Dunn School of Pathology

Howard Florey (1898–1968) led the effort to carry out clinical trials of penicillin at Oxford's Radcliffe Infirmary in 1941.

at Oxford, one of the premier medical research posts in the country. The school had opened with great fanfare and funding just eight years earlier, but it had never quite lived up to its billing as a place for pathbreaking science. With Sherrington's help, Florey got the position and committed himself to changing the fate of the school.

In short order, Florey revamped both teaching and research at the Dunn School. Unlike Fleming, who preferred to work alone or with a few collaborators that he chose himself, Florey saw the value of gathering researchers with different skills into teams, allowing each to focus on solving small pieces of large puzzles, and then offering them only general directions. The team approach would prove to be essential to work on penicillin.

Before any new work could begin, however, Florey had to address another problem that would bedevil him for years: money. As opposed to labs elsewhere, particularly in Germany, English labs in nearly all scientific disciplines were chronically pinched for supplies. The famed physicist Ernest Rutherford summed up life in an English lab: "We haven't much money, so we've got to use our brains."

The pursuit of research funding became perhaps the most important of all Florey's projects. While the estate of William Dunn, a London banker and philanthropist, provided the money to build and equip the school, there was no endowment to run it. There was little in the budget for anything beyond Florey's own salary, which was hardly plush. Florey even prohibited staff and students from using the elevator in an effort to save money. Eventually he banned the purchase of any equipment and even stationery.

Florey had not given up on lysozyme, even after eight years. But if he was going to make any progress he needed more help. He wanted to hire a biochemist, as that aspect of science was not his strong suit, as well as someone who could solve the countless problems that cropped up in a lab that was constantly short of supplies and equipment. He set out to find both, and the scientists he chose for those roles would together help transform medicine as we know it.

ERNST BORIS CHAIN

Like Florey, Ernst Boris Chain was an immigrant to Great Britain. The similarity ended there. Born in 1907 in Berlin, Germany, Chain was the grandson of a devout Jewish tailor from Belorussia and the son of chemist who founded a successful company that produced chemical salts. The company was prosperous for a time, but in the 1920s, as Germany's economy collapsed so did the Chains' family fortunes. After Chain's father died the family was forced to turn their comfortable home into a boarding house to make ends meet.

Despite the circumstances, the focus on scholarship and education remained intact. As Chain later remembered, "I was indoctrinated by both my parents with a maxim that was beyond discussion, that the only worthwhile pursuit in life was the pursuit of intellectual activities and any career which was not a university career was unthinkable."

Chain, whose long black curly hair and mustache gave him a striking physical resemblance to Albert Einstein, graduated from the Friedrich Wilhelm University in Berlin with a degree in chemistry and physiology. He early on developed an interest in using chemistry to explain biological phenomena, and he moved toward the still relatively new field of biochemistry.

Chain had another passion: music. He was in fact nearly as skilled at the piano as he was at the laboratory bench. He even toyed with the idea of making a career as a concert pianist or an impresario who could arrange performances from great artists from around the world. But perhaps still conscious of his parents' wishes, and no doubt attracted by the consistent

Ernst Boris Chain (1906–1979) arrived in England as a refugee from Nazi Germany in 1933. In 1939, he joined Florey's team and made vital contributions to the work on penicillin.

paychecks of an academic career, he in the end chose science, earning a doctoral degree in 1930.

Yet Chain brought to science an "artistic temperament," according to Gwyn Macfarlane, who worked with him and later wrote biographies of both Fleming and Florey: "true inspiration and originality." The dark side of that temperament could be dark indeed, as Chain was prone to angry and sometimes violent outbursts. He referred to himself as a "temperamental Continental," pacing the lab, celebrating success and bemoaning failure with equal intensity.

A few years later after finishing his studies, Chain, "disgusted by the Nazi gang" as he later wrote, abruptly departed for London. He had almost no money, and no prospects—an uncle living in London told him to forget finding work as a scientist and to take any job he could find. Chain, whose headstrong ways would later get him into countless squabbles, ignored him.

Fortunately for Chain, several British scientists, including Nobelist Sir Frederick Gowland Hopkins and J. B. S. Haldane, who was among the most influential scientists in the country, had read Chain's doctoral thesis on phospholipids, a major component of cell membranes. Haldane in particular was impressed and helped Chain secure positions first at London's University College Hospital and then in Hopkins's lab at Cambridge.

Hopkins was a firm believer that insights into chemical processes could provide answers to biological questions that had stubbornly resisted other scientific approaches. For example, how does snake venom cause fatal paralysis? Chain took up that question with the goal of explaining the structure of snake venom and the chemical changes it wrought upon nerve tissue. Instead of working with animals, as a biologist would, Chain separated various chemicals from animal tissue and then examined the effects of tiny amounts of snake venom. He eventually found that snake venom works by destroying an enzyme in the bite victim's nervous system that controls breathing.

That was exactly the kind of science that Florey wanted to be doing in his lab at Oxford. He believed that further advances in bacteriology demanded top-notch biochemistry. Florey recruited Chain to come work for him, and Chain moved to the Dunn School in 1935. He and Florey got along well, at least at first, but the good feelings would not last.

NORMAN HEATLEY

The final player in the antibiotic drama was the son of a Suffolk, England, veterinarian named Norman George Heatley. He was a modest man who received little notoriety for his work on penicillin during his life and even less after his death. Partly that was due to the oversize egos of Fleming, Florey, and Chain, and partly it was due to Heatley's own talent for minimizing his achievements. Heatley, for example, called himself a "third-rate scientist whose only merit was being in the right place at the right time."

That assessment was only half true. Heatley was indeed at the right place at the right time, and the world is far better off because of that bit of good luck. But he was certainly wrong in his assessment of his own scientific talents.

Heatley inherited one facet of those talents from his father, who liked to mend broken china by drilling holes into which he would insert minute metal pins. At a time when long, bumpy train rides were the main mode of transportation and most everyone brought along their tea pots, cups, and saucers, it was inevitable that a skilled repairman would be in high demand. Heatley's father earned a nice supplement to his income and passed along to his son the patience and dexterity needed for such work.

Heatley studied biochemistry at Cambridge, and like Chain he caught the attention of Frederick Gowland Hopkins. Heatley wrote his doctoral dissertation on a relatively new

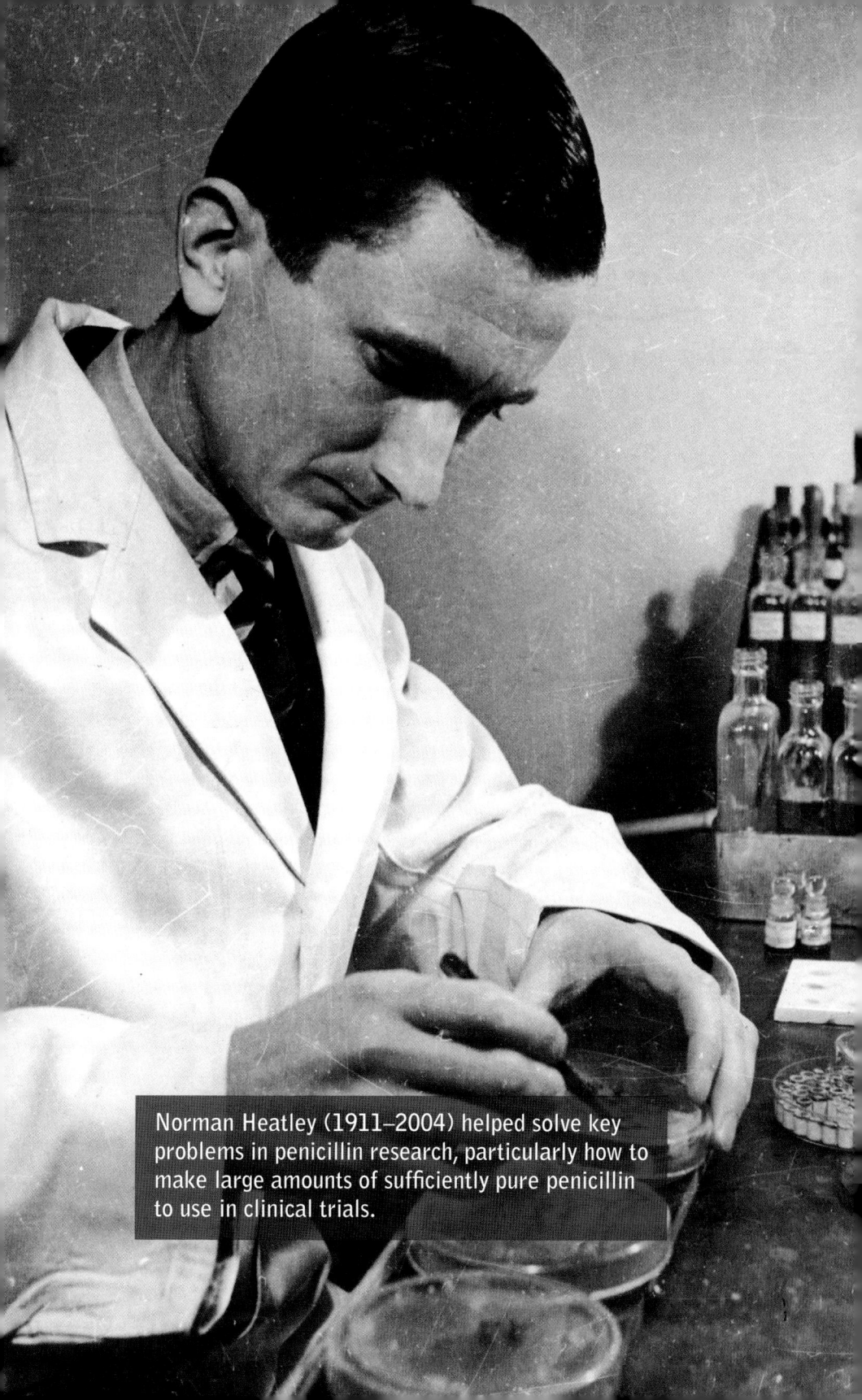

Norman Heatley (1911–2004) helped solve key problems in penicillin research, particularly how to make large amounts of sufficiently pure penicillin to use in clinical trials.

field called microchemistry, which uses precise methods to measure the amount of elements like carbon and nitrogen in other substances. In short order, Heatley became one of the few scientists in Britain who had mastered the necessary procedures.

Chain also noticed Heatley's work and especially his skill as an experimenter. He recommend Heatley to Florey for a job as his assistant, working on research Chain was beginning on the metabolism of cancerous tumors. To complete that work, they needed to measure the chemical activity of tiny fragments of tumor cells, but no such piece of equipment existed. So Heatley designed and built one himself, from parts he made and others he found lying around the lab. Its design and execution were so original that it can now be found in the London Science Museum. When World War II began a few years later and resources became even harder to find, Heatley's skill at laboratory improvisation would become even more crucial.

Heatley, typically shy and reluctant to seize the spotlight, and the talkative and ambitious Chain made an odd couple. There were professional differences as well. Heatley was a careful experimenter, whose detailed notes on every step and procedure would turn out to be invaluable later in the effort to produce large amounts of penicillin. Chain, on the other hand, was freewheeling in the lab, taking few notes and often leaping from idea to idea. That could lead to important insights, but someone else would have to come along and figure out how to design and run the experiments that would prove or disprove those insights. More often than not, that someone was Norman Heatley.

The differences in their background would cause difficulties. The German academic and research system in which Chain had been trained demanded that the senior scientist on a project be able to run the lab as he saw fit, without question from the junior staff. Chain expected this kind of deference from Heatley. But the English system, especially as implemented by Howard Florey, was more egalitarian. Heatley began to think that he, not Chain, actually had a better grasp of practical aspects of their research. While Heatley was unfailingly polite, even deferential, the relationship between he and Chain, and between Chain and Florey, began to fray.

While Chain and Florey would often have arguments that rattled the laboratory walls, Heatley kept his dissatisfaction to himself. His unwillingness to seek public acknowledgement of his work, even though he was quite aware of his own contributions, meant that he would become the forgotten man in the history of penicillin.

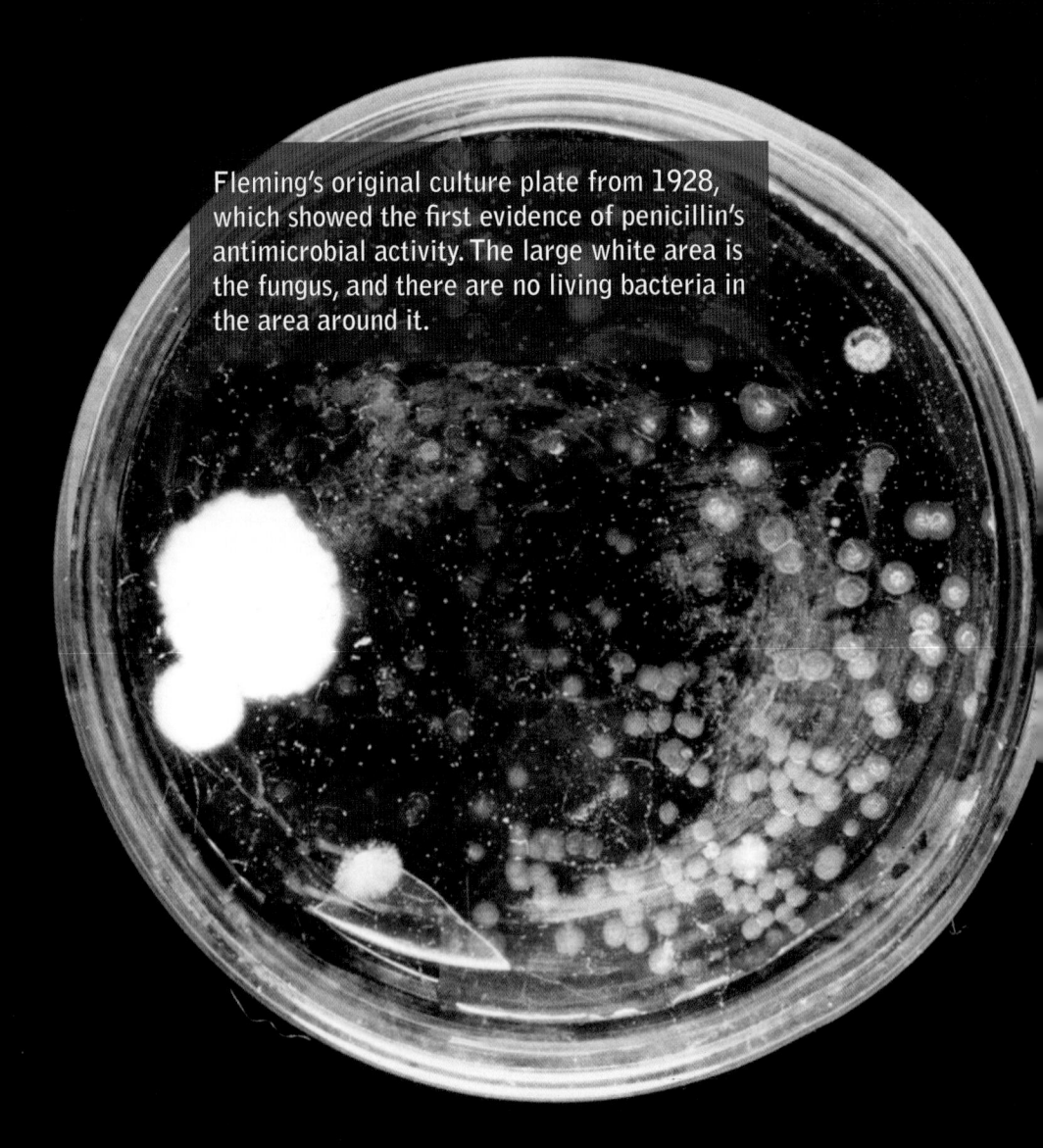

Fleming's original culture plate from 1928, which showed the first evidence of penicillin's antimicrobial activity. The large white area is the fungus, and there are no living bacteria in the area around it.

CHAPTER 4

The Discovery of Penicillin

The story of how Alexander Fleming discovered penicillin is among the most famous in the history of science. It has become almost mythical. But a good bit of that story may be wrong, and it is without a doubt incomplete. The real story, as is often the case, is more complicated and interesting.

A COMMON RETELLING

Here is the standard version of the story: in 1927, Fleming began research on *Staphylococcus aureus,* a bacterium that was particularly troublesome to humans and on which he was a renowned expert. He grew the bacteria in covered petri dishes, but he would have to remove the covers every now and then to get a closer look at the growing colonies of bacteria.

In the summer of 1928, Fleming opened one of his petri dishes for a few seconds, replaced the cover, and set it aside in a pile with two or three dozen others. Then he left on vacation. Some time after he returned to the lab in late August, Fleming looked over what he had left behind, making notes on the petri dishes one by one and stacking them in a tray of disinfectant to be cleaned.

By the mid-1940s, penicillin was widely available and a popular remedy for many ailments. Overuse of the drug quickly became a problem.

While he was doing this, a colleague came by to chat and see what Fleming was working on. He was about to hand over one of the dishes when something caught his eye. The dish had some blue-green mold on it, a common and annoying occurrence in a bacteriology lab. But when he looked more closely Fleming noticed that there were no living bacteria in the area immediately surrounding the mold, just dead, transparent cells.

Fleming did not shout "Eureka!" Just as he had been when he first noticed the effect of lysozyme seven years earlier, Fleming was terse: "That's funny," was all he said. But this was the moment of discovery. A mold spore had blown in through an open window on that warm summer afternoon, something in the mold had killed the bacteria, and all that was left to do was to isolate whatever it was and turn it into a drug. A neat and tidy story.

Separating Fact from Fiction

There are a few problems with the way that story has come down to us over the years. First of all, there is nothing in Fleming's notebooks from the day he first saw the mold growing in his petri dish. No one can say for certain what day it was. The first mention of penicillin comes some two months later, in reference to a formal experiment, not a casual observation. Fleming did not write up the standard version of the story until 1944, sixteen years after it happened.

Then there is the source of the contamination. It was indeed warm that summer in London, but no credible bacteriologist would work by an open window. That would practically guarantee contaminated samples. The way Fleming's lab was set up, with wide laboratory benches running the length of the room immediately below the windows, it would have been nearly impossible for Fleming to open a window even if he had wanted to. He almost never did because the street that ran by the building was too noisy.

There is also a problem with the sequence that Fleming described. As he recalled it, he had cultured the colonies of *Staphylococcus* for a few weeks, popped open the top of the petri dish for a quick peek, and that was when the mold snuck in and began to grow. But for penicillin to kill bacteria, it needs to be established first. If the bacteria are already growing then they will inhibit the growth of the mold, not the other way around. Fleming also said he was away from the lab for more than a month; in that time the mold would have covered the entire petri dish, not just a few spots, and it would have been impossible to see its effect on bacteria.

The REAL STORY

So what actually happened? Several scientists have attempted to piece the actual sequence together, and a few things seem clear.

The first is the source of the mold. It did not blow in off the street. But there were indeed billions of spores in the air of Fleming's lab. Just one floor below, an expert on molds was growing many different varieties, among them *Penicillium notatum,* the species that fortuitously landed in Fleming's petri dish. While modern labs have ventilation hoods to keep things like mold spores out of the equipment as well as out of the eyes and lungs of the scientists, at that time there was no way to stop the lighter-than-air spores from floating up the stairways and elevator shaft to Fleming's lab door, which he liked to keep open.

Luck played a large part in Fleming's discovery. His usual practice was to put the petri dishes streaked with bacteria in an incubator set to 38 degrees Celsius (about 100 degrees Fahrenheit). That is ideal for *Staphylococcus* to grow rapidly, but mold cannot grow at all at that temperature. So under normal circumstances, Fleming would have no mold colonies, and no dying bacteria. But since he was going on vacation, he decided that the bacteria would grow well enough while he was away, and he left the dishes on the counter instead.

Then another bit of luck: the warm summer turned cool, rising above 68 degrees Fahrenheit (20 degrees Celsius) only twice while Fleming away. That made for perfect conditions for mold, and terrible conditions for bacteria, so the mold could grow while the bacteria were inhibited.

Then still more luck: just the right kind of mold settled on that petri dish with just the right kind of bacteria. Of all the thousands of mold species in the world, and the dozens that were growing in the lab just below Fleming's, very few produce substances that can kill bacteria. Not even all types of *Penicillium notatum* do so; one specific and rare variant had to find its way up the stairs and in the door. And not all bacteria are susceptible; many are completely immune to penicillin's effects. If Fleming had been interested in any of those rather than *Staphylococcus*, which was particularly sensitive, he would have seen nothing of interest.

So a stray mold spore landed on an unincubated plate with just the right bacteria, the temperature dropped at just the right moment, Fleming returned from vacation just in time, and he took a second look moments before dropping the plate into a vat of disinfectant. The discovery of penicillin was almost as miraculous as the drug itself would later prove to be.

But there is still a puzzle left to be explained. If all those things happened exactly that way, why did Fleming wait two months before even bothering to write anything down about what he saw? One explanation, according to the science historian Robert Scott Root-Bernstein, is that Fleming was still looking for the effects of lysozyme. He found little lysozyme activity on the plate with the mold, so he set it aside.

Here is where Fleming made a key decision that takes the story in quite a different direction, away from the tale of accidental discovery that has become so deeply entrenched. Fleming was disappointed in the lysozyme activity but he decided to culture that mold anyway. This was Fleming's genius; he was not the first scientist to notice the curious characteristics of the *Penicillium* mold, but he alone pursued it. As the writer Eric Lax puts it, "Many stumbled upon penicillin; Fleming was the only one to look at what he tripped over."

After several weeks, Fleming began an experiment to test more rigorously for lysozyme. He put the mold on a plate with bacteria he knew were sensitive to lysozyme, as well as some *Staphylococcus*, against which lysozyme had no effect.

When he looked at the plate again, ten days later, he knew he had something exciting, something that could kill bacteria that were a cause of serious human disease. Now Fleming knew he must record his observation: "Therefore, mold culture contains a **bacteriolytic** substance for staphylococci."

The accidental discovery of penicillin thus may not have been quite so accidental. For whatever reason, Fleming sensed that the mold that had reached his petri dish was somehow important, and he pursued the question as a good scientist would: carefully and systematically. That he was looking for something else—lysozyme—did not in the end blind him to what he actually found.

Fleming then began to pursue the bacteriolytic substance in earnest and quickly gave it the name that would be forever linked to his own. First, he sampled other molds from books, cheese, bread, and even old shoes, but without success. Fortunately for Fleming, and for most everyone else as well, he kept the culture of the original mold growing, In fact, he maintained that culture for years, and much of the later work on penicillin began with samples from Fleming's lab.

Fleming next needed to learn if the substance that was killing the staphylococcus would do the same thing to other strains of bacteria. He took a petri dish and carved out a narrow canal through the agar. He placed mold broth containing penicillin into the canal, then streaked various bacteria—staphylococci, streptococci, **pneumococci** (which causes pneumonia), gonococci (gonorrhea), and meningococci (meningitis)—up to the edge of the canal. He knew that the penicillin would diffuse outward through the agar, so sensitive bacteria would not grow near the canal.

He found that penicillin acted powerfully against all of those bacteria but not against those that cause typhoid or influenza. It was also highly concentrated, which was good news, but highly unstable too, which would trouble Howard Florey and his team in years to come. Fleming also found that penicillin, unlike carbolic acid, did not damage white blood cells that help the body fight infection. With his wartime experience still in mind, Fleming had long sought an antiseptic with exactly these properties. Penicillin, he believed, would transform the treatment of infection. He was absolutely right about that, but not in the way he expected.

A NEW DRUG BEGINS to EMERGE

Fleming had made a dramatic discovery, but his own firm scientific beliefs kept him from making a miraculous one. Even though Fleming was a leading expert in treating syphilis, he did not test penicillin against the spirochete that causes that disease. He tested the toxicity of penicillin by injecting it into healthy mice and found no ill effects. But he did not test it in mice that had been injected with lethal bacteria. Had he done so, he would have been astonished that they did not die and penicillin as a drug might have been discovered years earlier.

But Fleming, along with his boss Almroth Wright, still labored under the belief that antibacterial drugs were impossible. He considered penicillin only as an external germicide. In later years, in fact, he used penicillin broth to clear unwanted bacteria from petri dishes during experiments. So what began as a contaminant, he then used to decontaminate.

Fleming's hypothesis was that penicillin destroyed bacteria through lysis—that is, by dissolving their cell walls. He published his initial observations of penicillin, to little interest. His first public presentation of his results, to London's

Medical Research Club in February 1929, did not go well. In fact, it seems to have made no impression whatsoever on the audience of scientists and physicians. Fleming later referred to the silence that greeted his findings at that meeting as "that frightful moment."

While Fleming continued working on penicillin longer than anyone else had, he too gave up intensive investigations on the substance after three years. Penicillin and its potential faded from view. Physicians and scientists would have to change their minds before Fleming's discovery could move from being merely interesting to being something that saved millions of lives. They would have to decide that an ingested or injected drug could be an effective treatment for a systemic infection.

Evidence Accumulates

In 1930, a pathologist working at a hospital in Sheffield, England, named Cecil G. Paine treated four infants and one adult man with eye infections with what he called "mold juice" from a sample of Fleming's own *Penicillium notatum*. All were cured. The babies had infections caused by gonococci and would have gone blind without the treatment. But Paine never published his results and later wrote, "I was a poor fool who didn't see the obvious when placed in front of me."

In 1935, another pathologist, Gerhard Domagk, began the research that would lead to sulfa drugs, the most important advance in medicine before penicillin. Dozens of new drugs were being investigated within a few years of Domagk's results being published. Paul Ehrlich's vision of chemotherapy from the turn of the century was finally on the verge of becoming a reality.

But there were false starts, too. Georges Dreyer, professor and chairman of the Sir William Dunn School of Pathology at Oxford, believed that penicillin was a virus and that explained its antibacterial action. Dreyer obtained a penicillin sample from Fleming in 1930, but when he discovered it was not a

The Sir William Dunn School of Pathology in Oxford, where Florey, Chain, and Heatley conducted their research

The Discovery of Penicillin 75

virus he abandoned that line of research. An aide, Margaret Campbell-Renton, kept the sample growing and was still tending to it five years later, when Dreyer's successor, Howard Walter Florey, arrived in Oxford.

OXFORD

Howard Florey did not set out to carry on Fleming's work on penicillin. Like Fleming, he was much more interested in lysozyme, and he asked Ernst Chain to work with him on determining how the enzyme dissolved bacterial cell walls. To start, Chain accumulated several hundred research articles on antibacterial action. Among them, by sheer luck, was Fleming's 1929 paper on penicillin. Florey had been the editor of the journal in which that paper had been published, but even he had forgotten about it by 1938.

    Chain was intrigued by Fleming's lysis hypothesis because he thought penicillin acted in the same way as lysozyme but against a far wider variety of bacteria, including some that caused human diseases. Then, in yet another stroke of the good fortune that seemed at times to hover over penicillin, Chain discovered that to find a sample of *Penicillium notatum* he had to go no farther than across the hall to Margaret Campbell-Renton.

    Chain and Florey decided that research into the biochemical and biological properties of antibacterial substances was a field ripe with scientific opportunity. They did not set out to find a drug that might be useful in the war that most everyone in Britain now believed was coming; instead they proposed basic research into how microorganisms produce antibacterial enzymes. They narrowed the field to three possibilities: *Penicillium notatum*, *Bacillus pyocyaneus*, and *Subtilis-mesentericus*. The fact that penicillin was hard to extract and unstable, yet potent, made it a good place to start for two scientists who relished a challenge.

A countercurrent machine, based on Norman Heatley's design, for purifying penicillin. Heatley assembled the original machine from spare parts he found around the lab.

The first step was to grow the most potent mold; only then could the Oxford team move on to questions about which bacteria were affected by penicillin, to what degree and by what chemical action, and whether or not penicillin was toxic to human cells and tissues. Growing and purifying penicillin sounds relatively straightforward: it is a mold after all, and mold usually grows readily under the right conditions. It turned out to be enormously complex.

Norman Heatley's many skills—carpenter, plumber, glass and metalworker, and above all improviser and problem solver—came to the fore in these early stages of the work on penicillin. Heatley developed a technique for determining the quantity of penicillin in a given sample that involved embedding small glass tubes into petri dishes of *Staphylococcus* and then measuring the circles of dead bacteria. The method would eventually be used hundreds of millions of times by biologists around the world, and it defined a unit of penicillin activity. Without those tools the research on penicillin could not proceed, and doctors would not have been able to give the drug to living patients.

Purifying penicillin was the next puzzle. Neither Fleming nor anyone else who had tinkered with penicillin had figured it out, but Heatley came up with a method based on a simple principle: two liquids of different densities, like oil and water, or in this case water and **ether**, will settle into distinct layers. Penicillin could be partially purified by mixing it with water to dissolve it, then with ether to get rid of impurities, but it would disappear when removing it from the ether.

Heatley found he could stabilize penicillin by keeping it near the freezing point and manipulating the acidity of the various solutions, making the water a bit more acidic, the ether a bit more alkaline. He filtered the mixture of penicillin and broth, then mixed it with ether, then again with water. If handled just right, the penicillin passed from the mold juice into the ether, then back into water without disappearing.

Heatley had to carry out most of this work in what was essentially a walk-in refrigerator, wearing a coat and mittens. He eventually built an automated system—called a countercurrent machine—from an old bookcase, glass tubing he made himself, various pumps, bottles, warning lights, and an old doorbell.

The final step was to freeze-dry the mixture, extracting a brown powder. The Oxford researchers found that it prevented bacterial growth when diluted to one part per million, far stronger than any sulfa drug. The scientists assumed it must be pure to be so potent, but in fact it contained about thirty different substances and was less than one-half of one percent penicillin.

In March 1940, Chain and Florey injected a mouse with penicillin and saw no ill effects. When they turned the mouse over they saw a pool of deep brown urine, which turned out to have enormous antibacterial power itself. They then knew that they had found a substance that could seep into tissues throughout the body, was not toxic, and was not destroyed by the immune system. That meant penicillin was certain to act against bacterial infections in a living organism. As Eric Lax puts it, "Penicillin suddenly looked not only like an interesting chemical, it looked like a drug."

Over the next few months, the researchers tested the toxicity of penicillin on cats, rats, rabbits, and mice. In another stroke of luck, they did not test it on guinea pigs, the one rodent that reacts badly to the drug. They found that penicillin did not kill white blood cells even at a concentration two thousand times the effective antibacterial dose. This was a huge advance: sulfa drugs were effective only at the point they became toxic, making them difficult and dangerous to use. Also unlike sulfa drugs, penicillin would prove to be effective in wounds where there was pus and other fluids, as well as tissue breaking down from infection.

Toxicity was one thing, effectiveness against actual infection was another. On May 25, 1940, Florey performed the experiment that Alexander Fleming had failed to do: he injected penicillin into a living creature with a bacterial infection.

As the test bacteria Florey chose *Streptococcus haemolyticus*, which causes such severe and fatal infections as septicemia (blood poisoning), meningitis, and scarlet fever. The scientists injected eight mice with a lethal dose of *Streptococcus*. An hour later, two mice were given a small dose of penicillin solution, and two more were given a larger dose. The first two mice were given four additional injections over the next ten hours.

Heatley stayed up all night to see the results. At 3:28 a.m., the last of the four control mice was dead. All of the treated mice survived.

That experiment marks the dawn of the antibiotic era. The next day, Florey called a colleague to report on the results. Usually reserved, he said, "It looks like a miracle."

FROM the LAB to the FRONT LINES

In one of history's remarkable coincidences, on the same day that scientists began an experiment that would save millions of lives, the war that would costs millions of lives took a dramatic turn for the worse. On May 25, 1940, the British navy, supported by a makeshift flotilla of lifeboats from liners in the London docks, fishing boats, yachts, barges, and pleasure boats, began a frantic effort to evacuate the surrounded British army from the beaches of Dunkirk.

Less than one month later, France surrendered. British prime minister Winston Churchill said, "The Battle of France is over. I expect the Battle of Britain is about to begin." These were the darkest hours of the war, perhaps the darkest of the twentieth century. Yet in Oxford a small band of scientists had reasons for hope, and anxiety.

A German invasion across the English Channel seemed likely. The scientists knew that if that happened, anyone doing research that could be valuable to the enemy would have to destroy it. That would mean destroying the single strain of *Penicillium notatum* known to produce penicillin, the very same one Alexander Fleming had discovered and that had been patiently nurtured for more than a decade. In something out of a spy novel, Heatley suggested the Oxford team rub mold spores into their coats. The hardy brown mold spores would blend into the fabric and would remain dormant but alive for years. The hope was that at least one of the scientists would survive and escape to the United States, where the work on penicillin could be completed.

In the meantime, the Germans began to bomb London, but Oxford was spared the worst of the onslaught. In July 1940, Florey, Chain, and Heatley gave fifty mice triple the dose of streptococci as the first experiment, then gave twenty-five of the mice doses of penicillin every three hours. All the untreated mice were dead within sixteen hours, while twenty-four of the treated mice were still alive ten days later. The one that died had an undetected and long-standing internal disease.

Finally, the time had come to make this miracle public. On August 24, 1940, the Oxford researchers published a historic paper in a British scientific journal, *The Lancet*. In that two-page paper, in the sober, understated language of science, they offered compelling evidence that penicillin was not toxic and was the most powerful antibacterial agent ever made.

The importance of penicillin was clear. Yet it would be nine months before any pharmaceutical company expressed any interest. While the scientists believed the drug could be tried in humans before its structure was fully understood, the drug companies thought that was risky and at the same time worried that knowing the structure might also reveal new methods of making the drug more efficiently. The companies were unwilling to invest in building large fermentation plants to grow mold that might quickly become obsolete. It would later

Women were largely excluded from jobs in science and industry in the 1940s, but they played important roles in the development of penicillin.

turn out that a peculiarity of penicillin's chemical structure would make it extremely difficult to synthesize in the lab.

Even though drug companies did not leap at the chance to make penicillin, Florey and the others knew that their project had changed from fundamental research to clinical trials. Britain was at war, and infected wounds were the biggest killer, as in all wars. So Florey violated a long-held tradition in Britain that universities do not get into the manufacturing business. He established what was essentially a small penicillin factory. Rather than build a single large factory that the Germans could bomb, penicillin was produced in every kind of facility, using whatever equipment was at hand. Eventually, basement labs all over Britain would produce penicillin.

The production method was complex. It required a medium to grow the mold, then a process to extract the penicillin from the fluid, which meant chilling the solution to the freezing point, then rolling the glass bottles with the mixture. Norman Heatley rummaged around the country for biscuit tins to grow mold and also used pie tins, bed pans, and even old gas cans.

Florey and his colleagues needed more than just containers; they needed people, but there were not enough men to do the rolling because of the war. Breaking another taboo, the team recruited women to roll the glass bottles back and forth in a freezing room for eight hours a day. They became known as "the penicillin girls": Ruth Callow, Claire Inayat, Megan Lancaster, Betty Cooke, Peggy Gardner, and Patricia McKegney. Several were under eighteen when they started. They earned £1 per week, equivalent to about $20 today.

The FIRST PATIENTS

The first human patient to receive penicillin was a man at Columbia Presbyterian Hospital in New York named Aaron Alston, who was suffering from bacterial endocarditis, a rare and usually fatal infection of the heart or its valves. His physician, Dr. Martin Henry Dawson, had read the paper in *The Lancet* and had immediately begun to purify penicillin. Unfortunately, he could produce neither the quantity nor the quality of the drug that he needed, and Alston died.

Even so, when Dawson reported on the drug some months later it generated bold headlines: "Giant Germicide Yielded by Mold," said the *New York Times*; "Germ Killer Found in Common Mold," said the *Philadelphia Evening Bulletin*. The pharmaceutical companies, however, were unmoved.

Florey and his team proceeded cautiously. They wanted to test the toxicity of penicillin in humans, and that meant finding someone to whom they could do no more harm: that is, someone who was already terminally ill. Elva Akers, a cancer patient at the Radcliffe Infirmary in Oxford, agreed to be a test subject. She experienced shivering and fever after the first injection, which turned out to be caused by impurities in the drug. The next batch was purer, and she had no bad reaction to further injections. The Oxford team did not know about the test in New York and thought this was the first time a person had been given penicillin.

Florey, Chain, and Heatley continued treating patients, including an Oxford police constable who had scratched his face while working in his rose garden and developed staph and strep infections. After five days of treatment, he seemed well on his way to recovery, but then the supply of penicillin ran out and he died. It was by now clear that successful treatment with penicillin meant treating patients until all signs of infection were gone, not just until they showed signs of clinical improvement.

In order to convince a pharmaceutical company to invest in large-scale production, the Oxford team would need enough penicillin to treat dozens of patients, not just a handful here or there. In the first eighteen months of experimental treatments, the Oxford team had used four million units of penicillin on six patients—what is now a single daily dose for one person. The

Industrial-scale production of penicillin began in the early 1940s. Drug companies in the United States made 21 billion units of penicillin in 1943, and that jumped to more than 6.8 trillion units in 1945.

best they had managed was two units of penicillin per milliliter of mold filtrate, and as much as 60 percent of that could be lost during extraction. At that rate, they would need over five hundred gallons of filtrate to treat a single serious infection.

They badly needed to increase the production of penicillin, but during the early years of the war manufacturing anything in England was next to impossible. Everything was rationed. So Florey and Heatley flew to the United States in June 1941, bringing samples with them in jars, along with the spores they had rubbed into their coats.

Florey and Heatley met with Robert Coghill, head of the fermentation division of the Department of Agriculture's Northern Regional Research Lab in Peoria, Illinois. Coghill suggested that deep culture fermentation, such as that used in brewing beer, would help: instead of growing only on the surface of the medium, in deep culture mold grows beneath the surface as well, greatly increasing the yield. It would turn out to be one of the two most important contributions that American scientists would make to the development of penicillin.

The other breakthrough was finding a type of mold that produced more penicillin than *Penicillium notatum*. An expert in fungi named Kenneth B. Raper had been testing soil samples from all over the world that were flown in by the US Army, and he asked his assistant, Mary Hunt, to bring back all the moldy fruit she could find from the local market. After testing dozens of molds they found a mold called *Penicillium chryosegenum* growing on a cantaloupe. It produced more penicillin and grew well under deep fermentation. From then on, Mary Hunt was known as Moldy Mary.

Florey continued pressing pharmaceutical companies to take on large-scale production of penicillin, and by the fall of 1941, interest began to grow. Five companies signed on to the project, and in March 1942, enough high-quality penicillin was on hand to carry out the first clinical trial in the United States. Howard Florey authorized the release of half of the entire supply then available—it amounted to about a teaspoon—to treat a single patient. In Connecticut, Anne Miller was suffering from blood poisoning that had developed following a miscarriage, an all-too-common and usually fatal complication.

All other treatments had failed. Miller's doctors administered a small dose of penicillin and waited. When she had no obvious adverse reaction they gave her a second, larger dose, and then still more every four hours. In less than twenty-four hours, her temperature, which had gotten as high as 106 degrees Fahrenheit (41.1 degrees Celsius), was back to normal for the first time in a month and the bacterial infection in her blood was gone. A month later, she went home from the hospital. She died in 1999, at age ninety.

For the first time, penicillin had saved a life.

Over the next year, twenty-one more companies joined the original five that had been producing penicillin in the United States, supported by the government's War Production Board. Production skyrocketed. In the first five months of 1943, those companies produced four hundred million units of penicillin, enough to treat nearly two hundred severe cases; in the following seven months, just over twenty billion units were produced. By the end of 1943, production of penicillin was one of the US War Department's highest priorities.

The year 1943 was important for penicillin and its soon-to-be-discovered relatives for another reason as well: they got a name. Selman A. Waksman, a microbiologist at Rutgers University in New Jersey, combined two words with Latin and Greek roots that meant "against" and "life." The age of the antibiotic had officially begun.

Scientific advances have led to the discovery of dozens of antibiotics, but the pipeline of new drugs may be drying up.

CHAPTER 5

A Post-Antibiotic Era?

Once the miracle of penicillin became clear, the race to claim credit for the discovery was on. Alexander Fleming had a head start, thanks to his friend Almroth Wright. In 1942, Wright wrote a letter to the *Times* of London in 1942 declaring "the laurel wreath for this discovery" belonged to Fleming. Florey, in contrast, was shy of publicity because he found it distasteful and because he worried that too much enthusiasm would be a problem until they had produced large quantities of penicillin. So it was Fleming's name that the public began to associate most firmly with the drug. That association would prove to be unshakeable.

FAME and OBSCURITY

Fleming in short order became perhaps the most famous man of science in the world. His photo graced the cover of *Time* magazine in May 1944, above a headline that claimed penicillin would "save more lives than war could spend." He would eventually receive honorary doctorates from around the world, dozens of prizes and medals, and memberships in important professional societies. In 1949, Fleming was even made an

By the end of his life, Fleming (*left*) was among the most decorated and beloved scientists in the world, the recipient of dozens of awards and honorary degrees.

honorary member of the Kiowa tribe in Oklahoma and given the name Chief Doy-Gei-Tuan, "Maker of Great Medicine."

Still, those most knowledgeable about the development of penicillin were well aware of the contributions of Howard Florey and his team at Oxford. Both Fleming and Florey were knighted by King George VI in June 1944—though of course Fleming dominated the headlines. Ernst Chain would be knighted as well, but not until 1969.

The most famous award, however, remained to be decided. The Nobel Prizes were put on hold in 1940 because of the war, but in 1944 rumors began to circulate that they would be restarted the next year. The other rumor was that Fleming, and Fleming alone, would be given the prize for medicine for discovering penicillin.

After long deliberations, the Nobel Committee in Stockholm, Sweden, awarded the 1945 prize in medicine jointly to Fleming, Florey, and Chain. Norman Heatley was not mentioned. Further misunderstandings of the discovery remained. The headline in the *New York Times* announcing the award read: "Fleming and Two Co-Workers Get Nobel Award for Penicillin Boon." They were of course not coworkers in any sense of the word, but the story of the heroic scientist and his accidental discovery was too powerful to overcome.

Fleming had one more important contribution to make to the penicillin story. It came during his Nobel lecture on December 11, 1945. After reviewing how he first stumbled upon penicillin, he ended with a remarkably prescient observation:

> But I would like to sound one note of warning. Penicillin is to all intents and purposes non-poisonous so there is no need to worry about giving an overdose and poisoning the patient. There may be a danger, though, in underdosage. It is not difficult to make microbes resistant to

penicillin in the laboratory by exposing them to concentrations not sufficient to kill them, and the same thing has occasionally happened in the body.

The time may come when penicillin can be bought by anyone in the shops. Then there is the danger that the ignorant man may easily underdose himself and by exposing his microbes to non-lethal quantities of the drug make them resistant. Here is a hypothetical illustration. Mr. X. has a sore throat. He buys some penicillin and gives himself, not enough to kill the streptococci but enough to educate them to resist penicillin. He then infects his wife. Mrs. X gets pneumonia and is treated with penicillin. As the streptococci are now resistant to penicillin the treatment fails. Mrs. X dies. Who is primarily responsible for Mrs. X's death? Why Mr. X, whose negligent use of penicillin changed the nature of the microbe. *Moral:* If you use penicillin, use enough.

Fleming put his finger precisely on a danger that would not fully emerge for decades but now has become so severe that today it threatens to plunge health care into a post-antibiotic era: resistance. Fleming would not live to see his prediction come true. He died March 11, 1955, from a blood clot in his heart. His ashes were interred in St. Paul's Cathedral in London, alongside such British heroes as the Duke of Wellington, Lord Nelson, Florence Nightingale, and Lawrence of Arabia.

RESISTANCE

Fleming was not the first scientist to foresee the problem of resistance. In 1940, Edward Abraham, who had been working closely with Florey and Chain at Oxford, found that organisms could over time become resistant to antibiotics. Abraham showed that growing *Staphylococcus* in increasing concentrations of penicillin increased the resistance of the bacteria a thousand times over.

The emergence of bacteria resistant to penicillin, and eventually many other antibiotics as well, is a textbook example of evolution at work. Any group of bacteria will have some genetic variation; some individual bacteria will be more able to withstand a given dose of a given antibiotic than others. The bacteria with the variant genes don't need to be completely immune to the drug, they just need to be slightly more likely to survive the first dose, or the fifth, or the tenth. If you do not use enough of the drug to kill even those slightly resistant strains, then those strains survive to reproduce. Now you have a population of bacteria that is more resistant than the previous one. Even if the difference is tiny, if you repeat that process many times over (as Abraham did in 1940), then eventually you will produce a strain of bacteria that is completely resistant to that particular antibiotic, and it will be useless as a treatment.

The mechanism of resistance to penicillin in most cases comes down to the ability to produce enzymes that can break up a specific part of an antibiotic's chemical structure. Abraham and Chain identified the first of these enzymes, called penicillinase, before penicillin was even in use. They found the enzyme in strains of *Escherichia coli,* a common type of bacteria that can cause gastroenteritis (sometimes called stomach flu), urinary tract infections, and other illnesses. Penicillinase rapidly spread to other bacteria, and scientists have since discovered many other enzymes that contribute to **antibiotic resistance** in countless bacteria.

In 2011, scientists discovered a key reason why bacteria were able to develop resistance so quickly: they have been doing it for thirty thousand years. Examination of the DNA of ancient bacteria shows that they were able to resist antibiotics many millennia before humans began using them as drugs.

Scientists found that the ancient bacteria already had the genes that make them antibiotic-resistant today. The discovery proved what scientists had long suspected: as fungi, algae, and bacteria evolved antibiotics to defend themselves against bacteria, the bacteria evolved in response. These organisms have been waging unseen chemical warfare for so long that they developed sophisticated weapons. Humans stumbled upon one set of those weapons—antibiotics—but were slower to understand the importance of the other set, or to appreciate that resistance to antibiotics is built deeply into the fabric of life on the planet.

The root of the problem, as Fleming anticipated in his Nobel lecture, is using penicillin or any antibiotic when it is not needed and not using enough of the drug when it is required. That problem was less likely when only physicians had access to antibiotics. That was not the case for very long.

Penicillin was so effective against so many diseases that once had been untreatable—among them anthrax, tetanus, gangrene, and diphtheria, as well as diseases caused by staphylococci and streptococci—that its use quickly spread. The mass production needed to supply the war effort also drove prices down: between 1943 and 1945, the prices of a million units of penicillin, enough to treat one average case, dropped from $200 to $6.

It was easy, and not all that unreasonable, for people (including many scientists) to believe that penicillin would solve every one of the problems of infectious disease. Then it spread far beyond doctors' offices and hospitals. People quickly began demanding it for mild sore throats, even though the common cold—the usual cause of a sore throat—is the result of a viral rather than a bacterial infection and thus cannot be treated with antibiotics. But patients demanded antibiotics, and physicians, though they knew better, often relented. The same pattern is repeated today.

The use of antibiotics in animal feed has led to the rapid spread of antibiotic-resistant organisms, which are now a major threat to public health.

Events outside the doctor's office also contributed enormously to the spread of resistance. The worst-case scenario is to have low levels of antibiotics circulating in the air, water, and soil, as that is guaranteed to kill off only the most susceptible bacteria and leave the more resistant strains alive to reproduce. But that is exactly what happened.

In the 1940s and 1950s, companies began putting antibiotics into such things as shaving cream and cosmetics. Even worse, pharmaceutical companies looking for new markets discovered that adding antibiotics to animal feed boosted growth in farm animals. The idea of using antibiotics as a production tool, rather than a medicine, changed the farming industry overnight. No one at the time was concerned with what it might be doing outside the animals, and in any event the choice for an individual farmer was obvious: increase profits and let others bear the cost of antibiotic resistance at some unknown time in the future.

NEW DRUGS

The emergence of resistant strains of bacteria was predictable, but in the years after the discovery of penicillin the progress against disease was so rapid that the hopes of countless people far outstripped the worries of a few scientists. The next target would be a disease that killed millions and against which penicillin was useless: tuberculosis.

Tuberculosis has haunted humanity since ancient times. Often called "consumption," it caused up to a quarter of all deaths and caused a high death toll in young adults in the nineteenth century. The only treatment, if it can be called that, was to isolate the patient in a sanatorium, which provided rest and sanitary conditions while protecting others from catching TB.

Only the relatively well off could afford a stay in a sanatorium or a long trip to the mountains, and half of those

Dr. Selman Waksman (1888–1973) discovered the first effective treatment for tuberculosis and was awarded the Nobel Prize in 1952.

who tried that approach died anyway. For the poor, living in crowded, dirty cities, the situation was far worse. Public health campaigns in European cities began to bring down the rates of tuberculosis infections toward the end of the nineteenth century, but progress was slow.

Robert Koch discovered the bacillus that caused tuberculosis in 1882. He examined the characteristic lesion of the disease, small nodules in the lungs called tubercles. In them he found a tiny rod-shaped bacterium that he called the tubercle bacillus. TB remains the common name for the disease, though the organism itself would eventually be renamed *Mycobacterium tuberculosis*.

Koch received the Nobel Prize in 1905 for his discovery, but his attempts to find a treatment failed. Fleming's early reports about the antibacterial activity of penicillin raised hopes about finally isolating a drug that would be effective against TB. Selman Waksman had long been interested in how soil microbes produce antibacterial substances, and in 1932 he began looking for soil microbes that could fight *Mycobacterium tuberculosis*.

Waksman's work picked up steam following the demonstration of penicillin's effectiveness. In 1943, Waksman and his collaborator, Albert Schatz, isolated a promising substance from a culture of a soil bacterium called *Streptomyces griseus*. They called it streptomycin. Unlike penicillin, it is effective against TB, and less than a year after its discovery the first clinical trials on tuberculosis patients were underway.

Streptomycin is different from penicillin in another important way; it is effective against both Gram-positive and Gram-negative types of bacteria, while penicillin is only effective against Gram-positive bacteria. Penicillin is thus known as a narrow-spectrum antibiotic, while streptomycin is a broad-spectrum drug, the first of its kind to be discovered. Broad-spectrum antibiotics are now the staple of treatment for infections. Waksman won the Nobel Prize in Medicine in 1952 for his work on streptomycin.

Further Findings

Now the floodgates opened. Nearly every pharmaceutical company in the United States launched massive screening programs to search soil, dust, and mold from every corner of the world to find the next antibacterial miracle. They were remarkably successful. In 1945, streptomycetes yielded a large family of antibiotics called tetracyclines, among which are some of the world's most fundamental medicines and the front-line treatment for diseases such as Rocky Mountain spotted fever, Lyme disease, chlamydia, and some types of pneumonia. In 1947, an organism from Venezuela called *Streptomyces venezuelae* was found to produce chloramphenicol, which became an effective treatment against meningitis, plague, and cholera.

Chloramphenicol was a landmark drug for another reason as well. In 1949, chemists determined its exact structure and learned that they would be able to make it in a laboratory. This was the first synthetic antibiotic. Many more would follow, opening an entirely new avenue for the development of effective medical treatments. After many years of work, scientists were eventually able to synthesize penicillin itself, but the process is so complex and the yields so small that the synthetic version has never found its way onto pharmacy shelves to replace that produced by mold.

While scientists were developing the techniques to create synthetic drugs, the search for natural sources continued in unlikely places, such as Italian sewers. In 1945, Giuseppe Brotzu, a biochemist who worked for the Public Health Service in Cagliari, on the island of Sardinia, went in search of an organism that produced an antibiotic effective against typhoid. Without the resources of a large drug company to screen thousands of soil or water samples, he had to be more enterprising. The incidence of typhoid fever in Cagliari was for some unexplained reason less than in the rest of Italy or Europe, so Brotzu reasoned that perhaps there were organisms in the city's sewers that had long coexisted with the typhoid bacillus.

Brotzu isolated a fungus he identified as *Cephalosporium acremonium* from Cagliari's sewers. He sent a sample to Oxford, where Edward Abraham isolated three separate antibacterial substances that he named cephalosporins. One of the three turned out to be even less toxic to humans than penicillin, and even more important, it was effective against penicillin-resistant strains of bacteria.

Despite all those important characteristics, it took nearly two decades to get from the Sardinian sewers to a drug that physicians could actually use. Since the first cephalosporin was introduced in 1964, however, more than five dozen derivatives have been developed to treat stubborn infections.

The list of antibiotics continued to grow, and many were variants of penicillin itself. Biochemists set out to understand how penicillin's structure led to antibacterial properties, expand the bacteria it would fight, and make it more readily absorbed in the body. This tweaking of penicillin's chemical structure led to "semisynthetic" (that is, partially man-made) penicillins and the introduction of methicillin in 1960 and ampicillin in 1961.

Ampicillin and a relative called amoxicillin were introduced in 1972, and amoxicillin is still in wide use, especially for respiratory and ear infections. Amoxicillin is also extremely important in the treatment and eradication of a bacterium commonly found in the stomach called *Helicobacter pylori*, which can cause ulcers and strongly increase the risk for stomach cancer.

KILLERS OLD and NEW

The sale of antibiotics became big business in 1950s, even as scientists began to sound ever more insistent warnings that overuse of the drugs would have serious consequences. Those warnings went largely unheeded until tragedy struck in 1967.

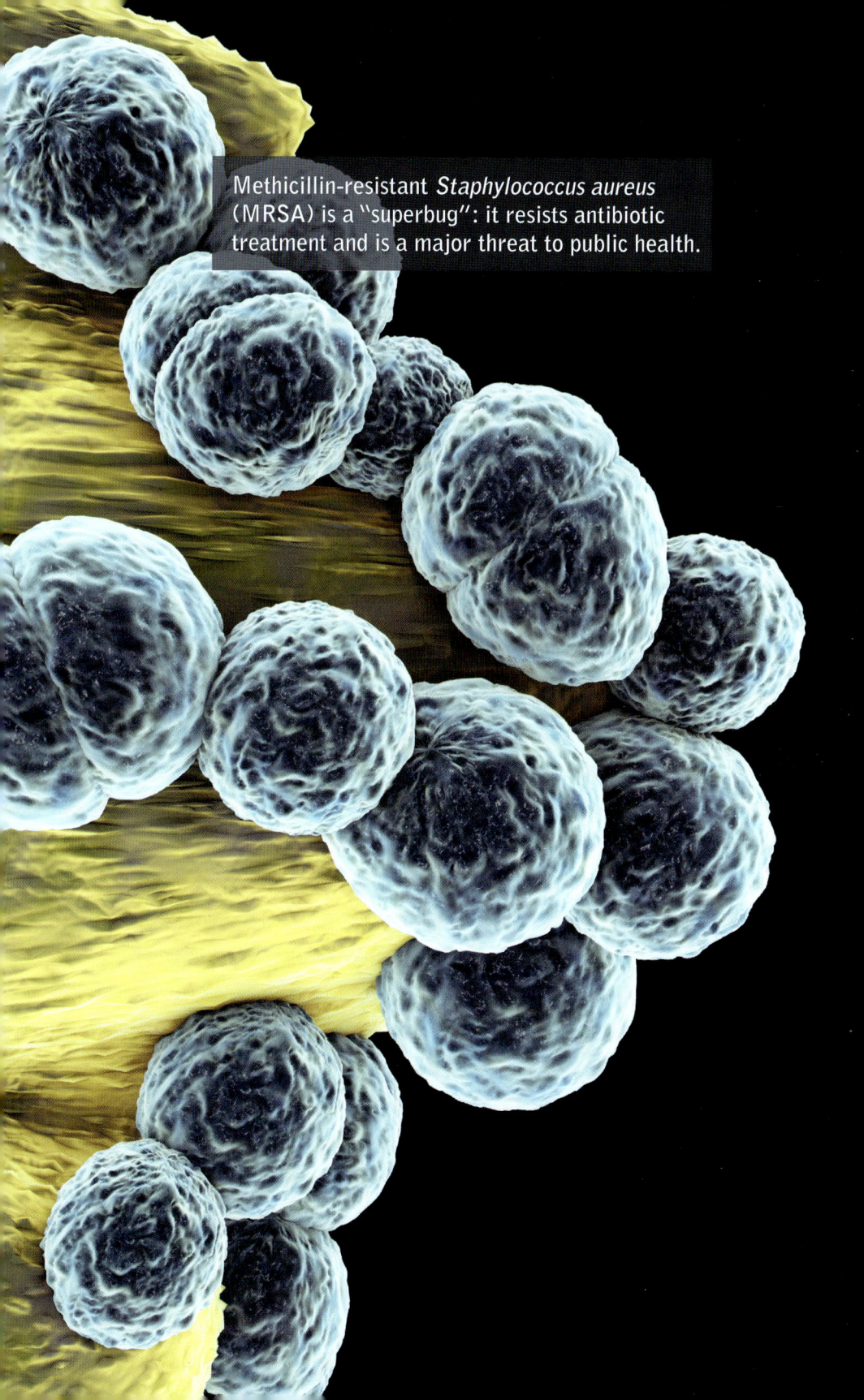

Methicillin-resistant *Staphylococcus aureus* (MRSA) is a "superbug": it resists antibiotic treatment and is a major threat to public health.

In November of that year, young children began to be admitted to a hospital in Middlesbrough in northeast England, suffering from upset stomachs, vomiting, and diarrhea. They were given the standard antibiotic, called neomycin, which Selman Waksman had discovered back in 1949. When they did not respond, doctors tried ampicillin, streptomycin, tetracyclines, chloramphenicol, kanamycin, and sulphonamides. Nothing worked. The doctors discovered that the children had been infected with an antibiotic-resistant strain of *E. coli* that they had never seen before, but by then it was too late. Eleven children died as a result of the infection.

The deaths of the children in Middlesbrough shocked the nation. The ensuing scandal brought new attention to warnings from scientists that antibiotic resistance had been developed in animals. The British parliament set up a committee to study the problem, which showed a link between use of antibiotics in animals and antibiotic resistance in humans. As a result, the government banned the use of four types of antibiotics in animals. The use of other kinds of antibiotics, however, continued to rise.

The number of organisms resistant to drugs that had been effective also began to rise. *Staphylococcus aureus*, for example, which can causes skin infections and food poisoning, was at first treated effectively with penicillin. By the late 1950s, however, penicillin was no longer effective, so doctors began to use methicillin instead. Just a short time later, methicillin began to lose its effectiveness, too, with the emergence of a bacterial strain called methicillin-resistant *Staphylococcus aureus*, or MRSA.

MRSA

MRSA is a particular problem in hospitals and nursing homes, where elderly residents are susceptible to infection. MRSA began to spread with infrequent outbreaks in Europe and

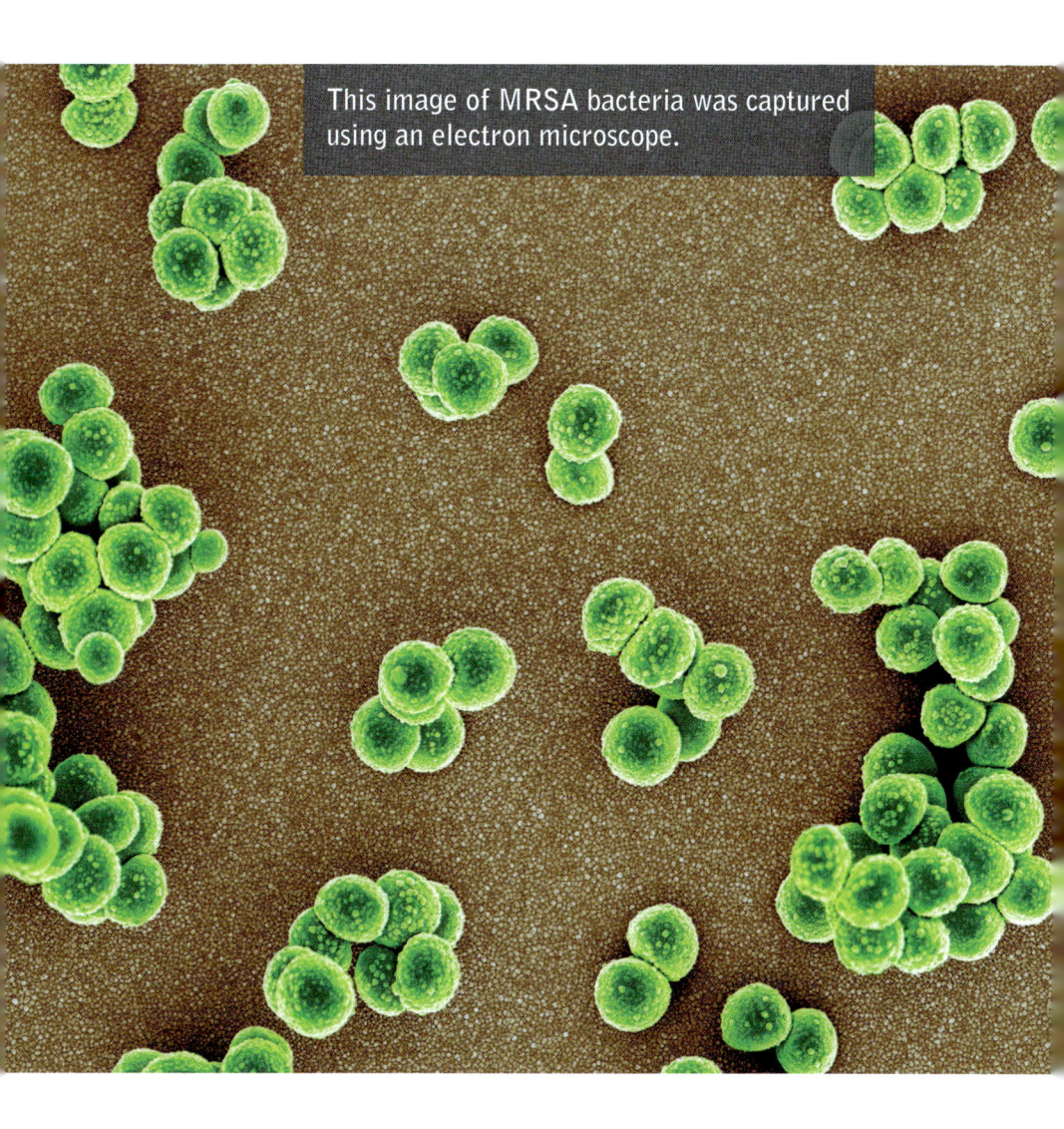

This image of MRSA bacteria was captured using an electron microscope.

A Post-Antibiotic Era? 103

Overuse of Antibiotics

Perhaps the biggest problem with antibiotics is that they have proven to be a little too good at their jobs. Physicians deployed them with stunning success against a wide range of bacteria that cause human suffering. But the drugs killed many other kinds of bacteria as well, and scientists are only now beginning to learn how vital many of those "good" bacteria are to our overall health.

The stomach and intestines, for example, host a large, complex community of bacteria—between five hundred and one thousand different species—that we literally cannot live without. In a healthy person, there are usually small numbers of potentially harmful bacteria, kept in check by the more numerous beneficial kinds. A course of antibiotics can wipe out many of those useful bacteria, upsetting the balance and allowing the more dangerous types to thrive.

One bacterium in particular, called *Clostridium difficile*, is a growing source of illness for exactly this reason. When antibiotics kill off normal bacteria in the gut it creates a void, and in some people *C. difficile* fills it. The bacteria produces a toxin that damages the intestine and can lead to severe diarrhea, internal bleeding, and, in severe cases, a ruptured colon and death.

Overuse of antibiotics has consequences far beyond any single microbe. Some scientists believe that early exposure to antibiotics in children can have life-long effects on metabolism and may contribute to childhood and adult obesity and asthma.

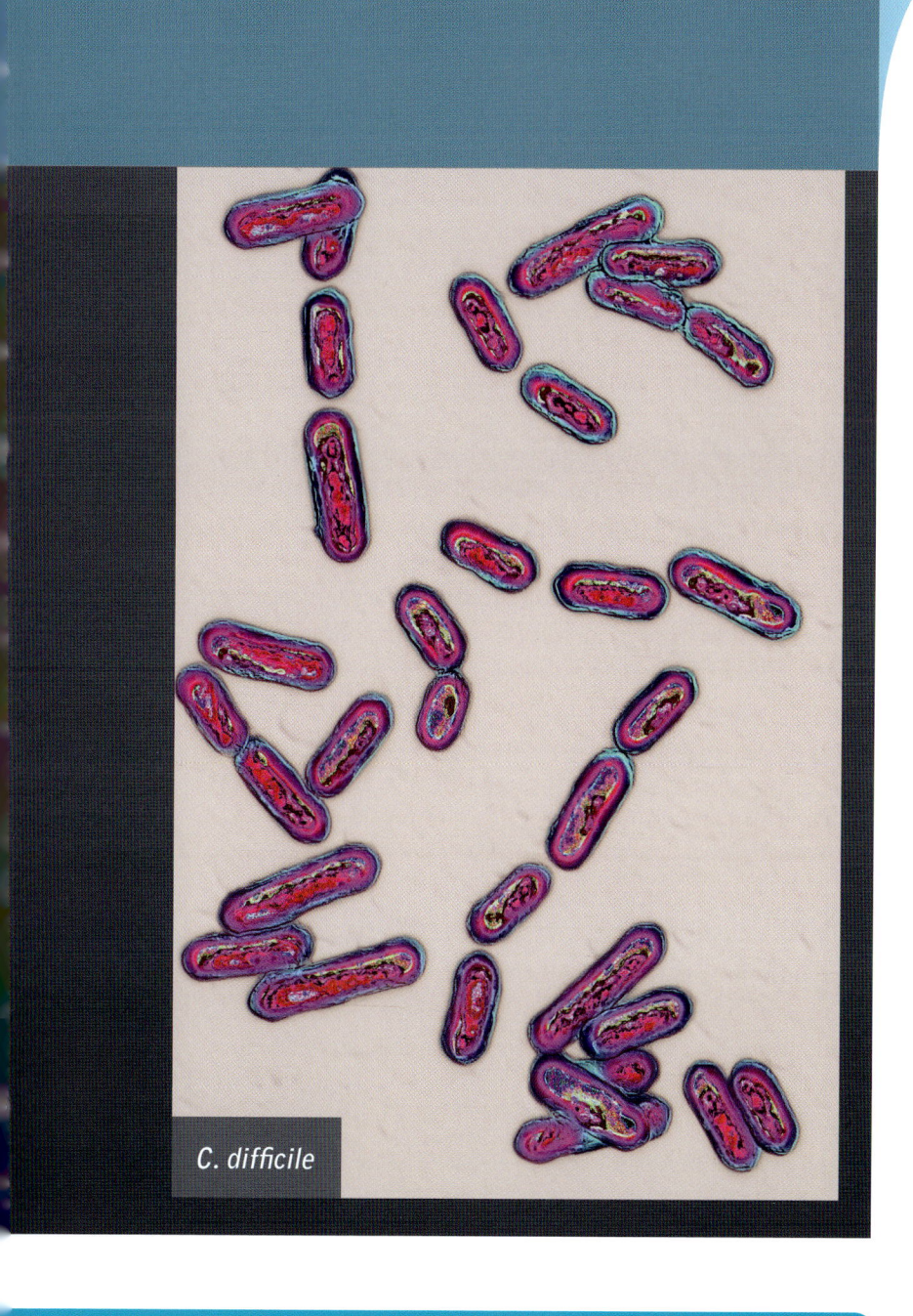

C. difficile

Australia between 1961 and 1967, followed by the first outbreak in the United States in 1968.

By 1974, 2 percent of hospital-acquired *S. aureus* infections could be attributed to MRSA; by 1997 that figure had reached 50 percent. In 2005, an estimated one hundred thousand Americans suffered severe MRSA infections, and nearly twenty thousand of them died.

The problem with MRSA has now become even more troubling. A hard-to-treat, hospital-based infection is bad enough. Then a variant of the original organism was found that could thrive outside of hospitals and cause even more serious infections in apparently healthy people. Those two strains have now merged into yet a third type, creating a "superbug" that often defies both diagnosis and treatment. About a third of all cases of so-called flesh-eating bacteria are caused by MRSA.

There is still one drug available to treat MRSA cases that resist everything else. This last line of defense, called vancomycin, was isolated in 1953 from soil collected from Borneo. It was hard to refine and to use—it is generally given as an injection rather than a pill—so it was not nearly as widespread as other new antibiotics. This may have helped lengthen the life span of vancomycin. While antibiotics resistance generally emerges within a few years of a new drug being introduced, in the case of vancomycin it took nearly twenty years before doctors began to see resistant strains.

VRE

Other troublesome bacteria have developed resistance to vancomycin, however. A group of bacteria found in the stomach and intestines called *Enterococcus* can cause urinary tract and blood infections, and many strains are now untreatable with vancomycin. By the mid-1990s nearly every hospital had seen cases of vancomycin-resistant enterococci, or VRE.

Vancomycin-resistant enterococci up close

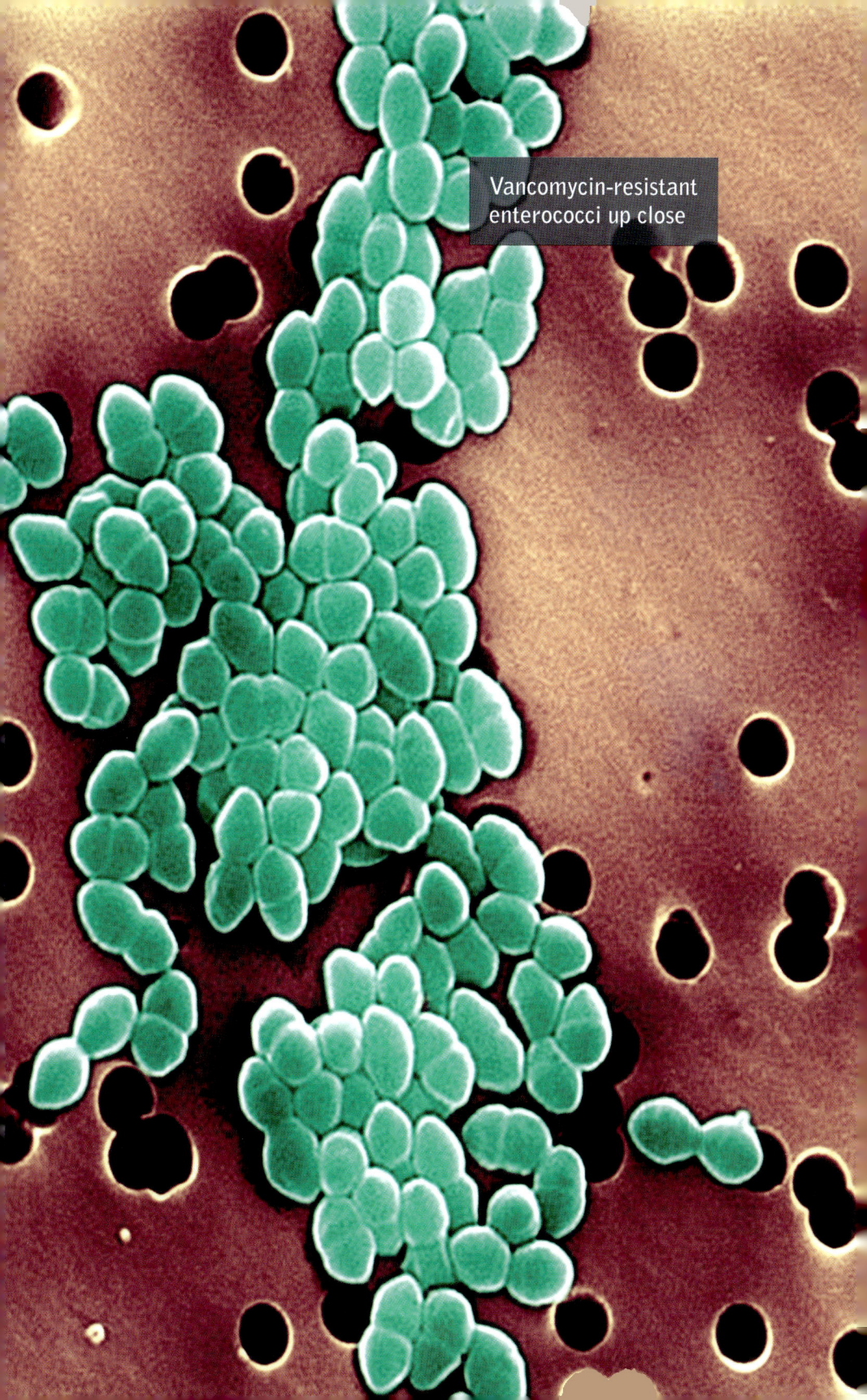

The emergence of VRE can be traced to a relative of vancomycin called avoparcin. While vancomycin is used exclusively in hospitals, in the 1970s European farmers began to treat their animals with avoparcin. That led to the development of resistant strains of enterococci that lived in livestock. Eventually, those resistant bacteria exchanged genetic material with bacteria that infect humans, and VRE was born.

Though the European Union no longer allows farmers to use antibiotics (including avoparcin) on their livestock, the practice is still common in the United States. The US **Food and Drug Administration (FDA)** launched plans in 2013 to gradually reduce farmers' use of antibiotics, yet many scientists warn of widespread danger.

The exact same pattern is being repeated with another drug of last resort, called colistin. Like vancomycin, it is not a new drug, having been introduced in 1959. Also like vancomycin, it was not used much at first because it can cause serious side effects, particularly damage to the kidneys. Since the drug mostly sat on hospital shelves, bacteria could not develop widespread resistance to colisitin, and it remained effective. But it is also being used in agriculture, mostly in China. A colistin-resistant strain of *E. coli* appeared in a patient in the United States for the first time in 2016.

The fear among doctors and public health officials is the emergence of bacteria that resist not just one or two antibiotics, but many. Such multidrug resistance can render doctors almost powerless. This has led to a worrisome surge from an old foe: tuberculosis.

More than ten million people were infected with tuberculosis in 2015, and nearly two million died from the disease. About six hundred thousand cases were multidrug resistant, and nearly 10 percent of those were an even worse form called extensively drug resistant that responds to even fewer medicines. Nearly half of the cases of resistant TB come from India, China, and the countries of the former Soviet Union.

The POST-ANTIBIOTIC ERA

The persistence of TB and the emergence of new challenges like MRSA and *C. difficile* suggest that the phenomenal success of antibiotics over the last seventy-five years or so may be at an end. While many of the drugs in common use will remain effective for years if not decades, we likely will never again see a time when so many new treatments come into widespread use so quickly.

The search for new antibiotics has slowed dramatically. Between 1983 and 1987, sixteen new antibiotics were approved for use in the United States; between 2008 and 2011 there were only two. No new classes of antibiotics to treat Gram-negative bacilli have been introduced in more than forty years.

There are several reasons for the slowdown in new drugs. First, we have already looked in all the obvious places, so the science behind new drugs has become increasingly complex. That in turn leads to the second problem: developing new drugs is expensive. Pharmaceutical companies must spend at least one billion dollars and years of effort to bring a new drug to the market, and antibiotics are not supposed to be taken on a regular basis. This means that companies have a low profit margin or even lose money creating new antibiotics.

With few economic incentives, the companies have either abandoned research on new drugs altogether or have focused on manipulating existing drugs, which is far less costly than searching for new compounds that work in entirely new ways.

Simply refining existing drugs will probably not solve the problem of antibiotic resistance. Scientists need a new approach. In 2016, researchers from Northeastern University in Boston made a discovery that may clear the way for just such a breakthrough by going back to the oldest of all sources of antibiotics: soil.

Soil teems with bacteria that scientists know almost nothing about. Estimates of the number of bacteria species in soil run into the billions—fifty thousand species in just a thimbleful of soil from your backyard—but only a tiny fraction of those can grow under laboratory conditions. The rest are unknown, and soil scientists call them "dark matter," borrowing a term from astronomy that refers to the unseen substance that makes up most of the universe.

Scientists in Boston have come up with an elegant solution to the problem. They developed a system called the iChip that enables them to grow bacteria in the lab, incubated in tiny bins full of their native soil. They began collecting soil samples from around the world. In 2011, soil from rural Maine yielded exotic bacteria that secreted a compound that was deadly to the anthrax and tuberculosis microbes.

Far more dramatic was the way the new substance, called teixobactin, worked. It destroyed microbes while leaving other living tissue untouched and did not lead to the development of resistance. Try as they might, the researchers could not breed bacterial colonies in the lab that were resistant to the new drug. This phenomenon had never been seen before.

Teixobactin kills bacteria by withholding two molecules that bacteria need: one to build cell walls, the other to keep their existing walls from breaking down. So teixobactin causes the bacterial walls to collapse, while at the same time preventing them from being rebuilt.

The chemical structure of the two molecules differs slightly across many different species of bacteria, but teixobactin attaches itself to parts of the molecules that are found in most or all of them. That suggests a reason why bacteria are slow to evolve resistance; to do so, they would have to change something that itself is the product of a long evolutionary process and has proven effective. Changing it would likely cause all sorts of problems.

Teixobactin, in short, is resistant to resistance. This is not permanent; evolution always wins in the end, but the hope is that it will take far longer for bacteria to develop resistance than is the case with all the other antibiotics now in use. That buys time, perhaps as much as thirty years.

Even more important, though, is the fact that the discovery of teixobactin emerged from a new way to explore the billions of bacteria that are all around us. Scientists turned that new way of exploring into a promising new drug quickly, and the hope is that many more such undiscovered compounds lurk in the dark matter of the earth.

Chronology

1675   Antonie van Leeuwenhoek sees microbes through a simple microscope

1721   Lady Mary Wortley Montagu and physician Charles Maitland promote variolation to prevent smallpox

1796   Edward Jenner vaccinates people against smallpox with the cowpox virus

1828   Christian Gottfried Ehrenberg coins the word "bacteria," from the Greek for "stick" or "staff"

1856   Louis Pasteur invents pasteurization

1861   Pasteur proves the principle of biogenesis

1865   Joseph Lister begins development of antiseptic surgical methods

1875   John Tyndall discovers *Penicillium*'s antibacterial properties

1876	Robert Koch proves that bacteria and viruses are the cause of disease
1877	Pasteur discovers that weakened bacteria would protect against later infection, thus describing the process of vaccination
1881	Pasteur demonstrates the effectiveness of his anthrax vaccine
1881	Alexander Fleming is born in Darvel, Ayrshire, Scotland
1885	Pasteur develops rabies vaccine
1910	Paul Ehrlich discovers Salvarsan 606, the first chemotherapeutic agent and first effective treatment for syphilis
1929	Alexander Fleming publishes the first scientific paper on the antibacterial effects of penicillin

1935	Gerhard Domagk discovers Prontosil, which kills systemic streptococcus infections when injected intravenously
1939	Rene Dubos isolates tyrothricin from soil microbe *Bacillus brevis,* later shown to contain the antibiotics gramicidin and tyrocidine
1940	Howard Florey and others publish a paper detailing the treatment of staphylococcus-infected mice with penicillin
1942	First human patient treated with penicillin
1943	Selman Waksman isolates streptomycin, the first broad-spectrum antibiotic
1945	Fleming, Chain, and Florey share the Nobel Prize
1949	Development of chloramphenicol, the first synthetic antibiotic
1952	Selman Waksman wins Nobel Prize for discovery of four antibiotics, including streptomycin
1960	Development of methicillin
1964	Development of Cefalotin, the first cephalosporin

1968 First US outbreak of methicillin-resistant *Staphylococcus aureus* (MRSA)

2015 Discovery of teixobactin, the first new antibiotic discovery in thirty years

ANTIBIOTICS

Glossary

anaerobe Any organism that does not require oxygen for growth.

antibacterial Anything that destroys or inhibits the growth of bacteria.

antibiotic A medicine that inhibits the growth of or destroys bacteria.

antibiotic resistance When bacteria become immune to medication that was previously effective in destroying them.

antiseptic Of, relating to, or denoting substances that prevent the growth of a wide range of disease-causing microorganisms. Unlike antibiotics, antiseptics are most often used externally.

atoxyl A compound of arsenic introduced as a medicine in the early twentieth century to treat sleeping sickness. It proved too toxic for human use but became the basis for a more effective drug, Salvarsan.

Bacillus A genus (*Bacillus*) of rod-shaped, Gram-positive bacteria; more generally, a bacterium that causes disease. Examples include the bacilli that cause anthrax and food poisoning.

bacteria Single-cell microorganisms that lack a membrane-bound nucleus, mitochondria, or any other membrane-bound organelle.

bacteriolytic Having the ability to destroy or dissolve bacterial cells.

biogenesis The idea that life arises from preexisting life and cannot arise from nonliving materials.

culture In biology, culture refers to the process of living things (especially microorganisms) in a constructed environment.

ether A light, flammable liquid frequently used as a solvent in laboratory experiments and previously used as an anesthetic for surgery.

Food and Drug Administration (FDA) A federal agency of the United States Department of Health and Human Services, responsible for the control and supervision of, among other things, prescription and over-the-counter medications, vaccines, cosmetics, and food safety.

Gram-negative Bacteria that do not take up the violet stain developed by J. M. C. Gram are called Gram-negative.

Gram-positive Bacteria that retain the violet Gram stain are called Gram-positive. Infections caused by Gram-positive bacteria respond better to penicillin and other first-generation antibiotics than do those caused by Gram-negative bacteria.

Haber-Bosch process The main industrial procedure for the production of nitrogen fertilizer.

leptospirosis An infection caused by bacteria called *Leptospira*. It is most common in tropical areas and infects seven to ten million people each year.

lysozyme An enzyme that is destructive of bacteria and functions as an antiseptic; found in tears, white blood cells, mucus, egg whites, and certain plants.

pneumococci *Streptococcus pneumoniae*, a Gram-positive bacteria named in 1886 for its role in pneumonia. It can cause many other kinds of infections as well, including bronchitis, ear and sinus infections, arthritis, and meningitis.

Prontosil The trade name for sulfamidochrysodine.

Salvarsan The first modern chemotherapeutic agent, first synthesized by Paul Ehrlich in 1907. Also called arsphenamine, or compound 606, Salvarsan was the first effective treatment for syphilis.

spirochetes Members of the phylum Spirochaetes, which contain bacteria with a distinctive double membrane and long, corkscrew-shape cells. Spirochetes stain Gram-negative.

vaccines Medicines that provide active acquired immunity to a disease.

variolation The first method of immunization against smallpox (*Variola*).

viruses Infectious agents that rely on living hosts to spread and do not respond to antibiotics.

Further Information

BOOKS

Brown, Kevin. *Penicillin Man: Alexander Fleming and the Antibiotic Revolution*. Stroud, Gloucestershire, UK: The History Press, 2005.

Friedman, Meyer, and Gerald W. Friedland. *Medicine's 10 Greatest Discoveries*. New Haven, CT: Yale University Press, 1998.

WEBSITES

Antibiotics Unearthed
http://www.microbiologysociety.org/outreach/antibiotics-unearthed/antibiotics-and-resistance/history-of-antibiotics.cfm

Explore a description and history of antibiotics from the Microbiology Society, a scientific research organization based in London.

Center for Disease Control and Prevention
https://www.cdc.gov

The official website of the government agency responsible for public health effort in the United States includes information about detecting new disease outbreaks and conducting research.

VIDEOS

"Alexander Fleming—Invention of Penicillin"
http://www.biography.com/people/alexander-fleming-9296894/videos/alexander-fleming-invention-of-penicillin-26300483971

Experts explain how Fleming's work has shaped the course of human history in this short video.

"What Causes Antibiotic Resistance?"
https://www.youtube.com/watch?v=znnp-Ivj2ek

This TED-Ed video provides an overview of antibiotic resistance and explains the dangers.

ANTIBIOTICS
Bibliography

Aminov, Rutam I. "A Brief History of the Antiobitic Era: Lessons Learned and Challenges for the Future." *Frontiers in Microbiology* 1 (2010): 1–7.

D'Costa, Vanessa M., Christine E. King, Lindsay Kalan, Mariya Morar, Wilson W. L. Sung, Carsten Schwarz, Duane Froese, Grant Zazula, Fabrice Calmels, Regis Debruyne, G. Brian Golding, Hendrik N. Polnar, and Gerard D. Wright. "Antibiotic Resistance Is Ancient." *Nature* 477 (2011): 457–461.

Fleming, Alexander. "On the Antibacterial Action of Cultures of a Penicillium with Special Reference to Their Use in the Isolation of B. Influenzae." *British Journal of Experimental Pathology* 10 (1929): 226–227.

———. "Nobel Lecture: Penicillin." The Nobel Prize Foundation, September 26, 2016. http://www.nobelprize.org/nobel_prizes/medicine/laureates/1945/fleming-lecture.html.

Francoeur, Jason R. "Joseph Lister: Surgeon Scientist (1827–1912)." *Journal of Investigative Surgery* 13 (2000): 129–132.

Harris, Henry. "The Discovery of Penicillin." Retrieved November 1, 2016. http://www.path.ox.ac.uk/content/discovery-penicillin.

Henderson, John. "The Plato of Praed Street: The Life and Times of Almroth Wright." *Journal of the Royal Society of Medicine* 94 (2001): 364–365. https://www.ncbi.nlm.nih.gov/pmc/articles/PMC1281610/.

Lax, Eric. *The Mold in Dr. Florey's Coat: The Story of the Penicillin Miracle*. New York, NY: Henry Holt and Company, 2005.

Macfalane, Gwyn. *Howard Florey: The Making of a Great Scientist*. Oxford, UK: Oxford University Press. 1979.

———. *Alexander Fleming: The Man and the Myth*. Cambridge, MA: Harvard University Press. 1984.

Markel, Howard. "The Real Story Behind Penicillin." PBS. Retrieved November 1, 2016. http://www.pbs.org/newshour/rundown/the-real-story-behind-the-worlds-first-antibiotic/.

The Nobel Foundation. "Sir Alexander Fleming—Biographical." Nobel Lectures, Physiology or Medicine 1942–1962. Retrieved November 1, 2016. http://www.nobelprize.org/nobel_prizes/medicine/laureates/1945/fleming-bio.html.

———. "Sir Howard Florey—Biographical." Nobel Lectures, Physiology or Medicine 1942–1962. Retrieved November 1, 2016. http://www.nobelprize.org/nobel_prizes/medicine/laureates/1945/florey-bio.html.

———. "Ernst B Chain—Biographical." Nobel Lectures, Physiology or Medicine 1942–1962. Retrieved November 1, 2016. http://www.nobelprize.org/nobel_prizes/medicine/laureates/1945/chain-bio.html.

Root-Bertstein, Robert Scott. *Discovering*. Cambridge, MA: Harvard University Press, 1989.

Schwartz, R. S. "Paul Ehrlich's Magic Bullets." *New England Journal of Medicine* 350 (11) (2004): 1079–80.

Sepkowitz, Kent A. "One Hundred Years of Salvarsan." *New England Journal of Medicine* 365 (4)(2011): 291–3.

Wade, Nicholas. "Researchers Find Antibiotic Resistance in Ancient DNA." *New York Times,* August 31, 2011.

Wilson, David. *In Search of Penicillin*. New York, NY : Knopf, 1976.

ANTIBIOTICS
Index

Page numbers in **boldface** are illustrations. Entries in **boldface** are glossary terms.

Abraham, Edward, 92–93
Akers, Elva, 84
Alston, Aaron, 83–84
amoxicillin, 100
anaerobe, 44
animalcules, 6, 14, 16
animal feed, antibiotics in, **95**, 96, 102
anthrax, 25–26, 34, 46, 94, 110
antibacterial, 45–46
antibiotic resistance, 93–96, 100–111
antibiotics
  discovery of, 5–7, 67–87, 89–91, 96–100
  disease before, 9–27
  naming of, 87
  overuse of, 100–102, 104
  synthetic, 99
antiseptic, 25, 42–44, 55, 73

Aristotle, 10
artemisinin, 11
atoxyl, 36–37

Bacillus, 25–26, 98
bacteria
  categories of, 35
  as cause of disease, 7, 30, 32, 34, 37, 40, 46
  discovery of, 6, 14, 16
  killing of with antibiotics/penicillin, 35, 46, 69–81, 104
  resistance to antibiotics, 92–96, 100–111
  Tyndall's study of, 30–31
bacteriolytic, 72
biogenesis, 10, 32
Brotzu, Giuseppe, 99–100
Burdon-Sanderson, Sir John Scott, 31

Callow, Ruth, 83
Campbell-Renton, Margaret, 76

C. difficile, 104, **105**, 109
Chain, Ernst Boris, 7, 49–50, 59–65, **60**, 76, 79, 81, 84, 91, 93
chemotherapy, 35, 38, 44, 46, 74
cholera, 12, 25–26, 99
Coghill, Robert, 86
Cooke, Betty, 83
countercurrent machine, **77**, 79
cowpox, 6–7, 19–20
culture, 25–26, 31, 56, 70–72

Dawson, Martin Henry, 84
Dioscorides, 11–12
disease
  early understanding and treatment of, 10–27
  germ theory of, 23–27, 32
Domagk, Gerhard, 74
Dreyer, Georges, 74
drug companies, 37–38, 81–84, **85**, 86–87, **88**, 96, 99, 109
Dunning, Richard, 20

E.coli, **8**, 93, 102, 108
Ehrenberg, Christian Gottfried, 16
Ehrlich, Paul, 35–38, 40, **41**, 45, 74
epidemics, 12, 15, 18

Erasmus, 36
ether, 78

Fleming, Alexander, 5–7, 25, 38, 44–47, **48**, 49–56, **51**, 58, 61–62, 67–78, 80–81, 89–92, **90**, 94, 98
Florey, Howard, 7, 49–50, 56–59, **57**, 61–65, 73, 76, 79–86, 89–91
Food and Drug Administration (FDA), 108
fungi, 16, 32, 86, 94, 100

Gardner, Peggy, 83
Gram, Hans Christian, 35
Gram-negative, 35, 98, 109
Gram-positive, 35, 98

Haber-Bosch process, 35
Haldane, J. B. S., 61
Harris, Henry, 50
Heatley, Norman, 7, 49–50, 62–65, **63**, 78–79, 81, 83–86, 91
Herodotus, 10
Hooke, Robert, 12–14
Hopkins, Frederick Gowland, 61–62
hospitals, **4**, 5–6, 23–25, 42, **43**, 44, 52–53, 61, 102, 106
Hunt, Mary, 86

Index 125

immunology, 32–34, 40
Inayat, Claire, 83

Jenner, Edward, 7, 19–20, **21**, 26, 29

Koch, Robert, 25, 29, 32, 98

Lancaster, Megan, 83
Leeuwenhoek, Antonie van, 6, 12–14, **13**, 16, 20
leptospirosis, 36
Lister, Joseph, 23–25, 29, 31, 42–44
lysozyme, 46, 56–58, 69, 71–72, 76

Macfarlane, Gwyn, 61
Maitland, Charles, 18
malaria, 11, 37
McKegney, Patricia, 83
medicine, early, 11–12
methicillin-resistant *Staphylococcus aureus* (MRSA), **101**, 102–106, **103**, 109
microbiology, 29–32
microscope, 6, 12–14, 16
Miller, Anne, 87
molds, 16, 31, 49, 55, 69–72, 74, 78, 81–83, 86, 99
Montagu, Lady Mary Wortley, 14–15, **17**

Noble Prize, 11, 34, 40, 49–50, 54–56, 61, 91–92, 94, 98

Oxford, 49, 56–58, 62, 74–81, 84, 91–92, 100

Paine, Cecil G., 74
Pasteur, Louis, 7, 16, 20–27, **24**, 29–34, 42, 50
pasteurization, 20–23, **22**
penicillin, 54, 58, **66**, **68**, 100
  discovery of, 31–32, 67–87, 89–92
  first patients to receive, 83–87
  production of, 64, 78–79, 81–87, **85**, 94
  resistance to, 92–96, 102
Penicillium chryosegenum, 86
Penicillium notatum, **28**, 31–32, 49, 54, **66**, 70–72, 74–76, 81, 86
Phipps, James, 19–20, **21**
pneumococci, 72
Prontosil, 38

rabies, 26–27
Raper, Kenneth B., 86
resistance to antibiotics, 92–96
Rutherford, Ernest, 58

126 Antibiotics

Saint Mary's Hospital, 5, 42, 52–53
Salvarsan, 37–38, 45
Schatz, Albert, 98
Sherrington, Charles, 56–58
smallpox, 7, 15, 18–20, 26, 36
soil, antibiotics in, 6, 11, 86, 96–99, 106, 109–110
spirochetes, 36–37, 73
Staphylococcus aureus, 67, 70–72, 78, 93, 94, 102, 106
streptococcus, 37–38, 46, 72, 80–81, 94
streptomycin, 98, 102
sulfa drugs, 38, 74, 79
syphilis, 36–38, 45, 73

teixobactin, 110–111
Timoni, Emmanuel, 18
Tyndall, John, 29–32
Tyndall Box, 29–30, **33**
tuberculosis, 40, 96–98, 108–110

vaccines, 7, 14–20, 26–27, 34, 42

vancomycin, 106–108
vancomycin-resistant enterococci (VRE), 106–108, **107**
van Helmont, Jan Baptiste, 10
variolation, 18–20
viruses, 74–76
  as cause of disease, 7, 16
vitalism, 34
Vuillemin, Jean-Paul, 32

Waksman, Selman, 87, **97**, 98, 102
William Dunn School of Pathology, 56–58, 62, 74, **75**
women in science, 76, **82**, 83, 86
World War II, 80–83, 86, 91
Wright, Almroth, 38–46, **39**, 52–53, 73, 89

yeasts, 14, 16, 20, 23, 32

About the Author

Jonathan S. Adams has been writing about medicine, medical research, and science for more than twenty-five years. Trained as a journalist, he covered the latest discoveries in a range of medical specialties before pursing a master's of science degree. He has written or edited five books on a variety of scientific topics. He lives in the suburbs of Washington, DC.